RUTHLESS POSSESSION

DARK ENEMIES BOOK ONE

ZOE DELANEY

"Weak men wait for opportunities. Strong men make them."
Orison Swett Marden

Rio

I LIVE FOR THE BUSINESS. I kill for the business.

Everyone says I'm an emotionless monster. And they're right.

That's why Danelli's standing in front of me now, delivering the news I've been waiting for.

My second-in-charge pushes his dark hair back out of his eyes. "We found the missing Carlotti girl. You were right all along, Boss. She's alive."

To hide our conversation, the thrum of DJ music, muted by the soundproofing in the offices of my club, rises up through the exotic African hardwood flooring, the background noise and hum of the crowd one of the advantages of the club's location.

I crave those sounds when I'm not in the office. They mask the emptiness inside me; the space where my heart should be. And the sophisticated women gracing the dance floor below provide endless fodder for my sexual appetites.

Most of them will do just about anything to spend a night with me... Gregorio Agosti, head of the combined Agosti-Carlotti crime syndicate.

All of them discover, too late, that my appetites are dark and rarely sated in a way that brings pleasure without the pain.

I stare at my second who has just delivered the golden opportunity I've been waiting for. I've been looking for Bianca Carlotti for the past seven years.

Mafia princess.

Loose end.

One I need to eliminate.

I don't trust myself to speak without betraying my excitement, so instead, I simply hold out my hand for the file clutched in Danelli's fist.

Emotion is a weakness in our world. My position is not so set in stone that I can afford to show even a hint of anything other than what they all expect: coldness. Dispassion.

But the photo on the front of the file Danelli hands me is not what *I* expect.

The woman has long dark hair, not immaculately styled but instead gathered into some kind of messy knot atop her head. Her brown eyes are crinkled at the edges, because the photographer obviously snapped her mid-laugh. A wide mouth with generous lips and a sprinkling of freckles across her nose give her an air of innocence.

She's wearing no makeup that I can discern, and her T-shirt above the jeans is gray and almost shapeless.

Is this really her?

Not that she would be aware of her heritage, necessarily, but surely, if it is the Carlotti girl, something of her birthright must remain. She looks nothing like the women who inhabit my world.

"Are you sure you got the right woman?"

Danelli flinches at my frosty tone, his shadowed eyes flicking to the photo in my now-clenched fist and his skin not tan enough to hide a sudden pallor. He *should* flinch. If his team got this wrong and raised my hopes for nothing, there will be dire consequences.

"Yes, Boss. A hundred percent. We took some of her hair and swiped her toothbrush. The DNA came back a match. It's her."

I turn away and pour a whiskey into one of the crystal tumblers from the antique set behind my desk, then take a couple of sips while I flip through the rest of the file and process the information therein.

Current alias: Bree Walker.

Current address: Franklin Park.

Place of work: Lots of Paws Animal Rescue Center.

A short bark of laughter escapes me. Not far from where she would've ended up if she'd stayed in the life she was born to. Only, she'd have been dealing with human animals instead.

Danelli's dark eyebrows lower. "You want her dead, Boss?"

I rest the tumbler against my lips, staring down at my desktop. Elimination of this final loose end would be the quickest and easiest option, but something stays my order.

3

I frown, not understanding my own motives.

Maybe I want to meet her before I have her killed.

Maybe I want to see if the innocence in her eyes is real. For her sake, I hope it's not.

Innocence brings out the worst in me.

"Not yet," I say slowly. Carefully. "Grab her and bring her to me. Do it before sundown tomorrow."

Bree

CLUBS ARE NOT MY SCENE, but it seems like Shelley's not going to take no for an answer.

"Bree, you *have* to come out with us tonight. It's your birthday. You've got no choice, girl!"

Shelley waggles her fingers in my face as we wait for Dave to lock up. The evening staff have already clocked in, but they'll go in and out the back entrance. The front is locked up tight every afternoon at four, when the rescue shelter closes to the public.

Which means I don't have any reason not to take up Shelley's invitation to celebrate my quarter century with espresso martinis.

"We can really dress up for once," she says, nudging Dave as he joins us on the sidewalk. "You coming too? Bree's twenty-five today. Tell her. She can't just go home and sit on the couch with a book like she always does."

Dave spears me with a look that seems unusually serious for a guy who values laid-back quiet time above all else. "You should do something other than work all the time, Bree. It isn't healthy."

"Ah…" I blink at the unexpected comment from someone I thought was just as introverted as me. "Don't you hate clubs and the night scene as much as I do? Traitor!"

He grins at me, squaring his shoulders. "I'll go if you do."

I release a sigh, but I've already decided. What the hell, why not? The incident with the spiked drink was three years ago now.

Besides, there's something in Dave's expression when he stares at me. Something new that gives me a gentle squiggle in my belly and makes me want to explore it further. "Okay. I guess you're both right. It'll be good for me to get out for once. I mean, twenty-five is pretty momentous, isn't it? All downhill from here, or so I've heard."

We're all still laughing when a sleek black car mounts the curb and pulls to a stop beside us.

"What the…" Dave drags both me and Shelley back out of its path, as two of the doors pop open and guys who look like twin gangsters jump out.

They're both wearing suits and have dark sunglasses jammed on their faces, despite the fact that the November weather is overcast and ready to drizzle.

But it isn't the redundant shades that capture and hold my attention.

It's the big black guns in their hands.

My mouth drops open, and my heart shoots up into my throat.

"Holy shit." The expletive leaves my lips involuntarily, and I stumble into Shelley, who clutches at my arm.

She's obviously just as terrified as me.

Is this some kind of attack on the animal shelter?

They don't look like activists. They look like caricatures of criminals. Really freaking scary ones.

Is it a daylight robbery?

My brain is going a million miles a minute, trying to figure out who they are and what they may want, and whether me and my two work colleagues are about to end up dead.

One of the thugs looks at the other. "Which is it?"

"Dark hair." The second one gestures at me.

Oh, hell. Shelley's a redhead, and Dave is a tousled blond.

Despite the guns, I open my mouth to scream, but one of the thugs shoves his hand roughly across my face, then picks me up as easily as if I'm a child.

Someone inside the car must pop the trunk, because I barely have time to struggle before I'm thrown in the back and the lid slams shut. I do start screaming then, at the top of my lungs, kicking and punching at every surface of the enclosed space.

I'm being *kidnapped*?

The trunk muffles Dave and Shelley's yelling and screaming on the outside, then a sharp pop, pop, pop sound strangles my voice and sends a wave of nausea rushing through me at the sudden silence from outside.

Oh my God oh my God oh my God…

Did they just kill my friends?

I realize I'm gasping and sobbing, and I wrap my arms across my middle, trying to hold in the panic.

This has to be some kind of sick joke.

A birthday prank that will end any minute, and result in me drinking a whole shit-ton of whatever cocktail gets handed to me to come down from the adrenaline rush.

It has to be a joke. This can't be real.

The car takes off, and I bump my head on something as we crunch down, presumably off the curb.

I hope that crunch broke something underneath the car. I

hope they leak so much oil the cops pull them over.

Cops. A thought penetrates my fog of panic. I recall seeing something on TV once about punching out a taillight if you ever find yourself in the unlikely situation where you're kidnapped and shoved in a car trunk.

Because, you know, facing that situation is so likely.

I hold back a burst of hysterical laughter, and shuffle my way to the back of the space, feeling for the taillight... There it is.

I make a fist and start to punch, realizing quickly I don't have enough strength. I need to kick it out.

I scream again, releasing all the fear of my situation, then find I can't stop screaming.

The vehicle swerves and then screeches to a halt. Before I can kick at the taillight, the lid opens, and the same guy who picked me up leans in, staring at me. "Shut the fuck up."

I don't even think, just launch at him with my foot, getting him square in the face.

He reels back, and then rushes forward again, the gun suddenly appearing in his hand. "You fucking little whore. You'll pay for that, bitch."

I freeze, staring at the tiny black hole as he shoves the weapon right up in my face. I've never seen a gun in real life, let alone been this close to one, until today.

It's all I can do to stop my teeth clattering as I fight to keep from losing it.

Without warning, he clicks a lever—the safety? And then he hits me with the barrel, right across my left cheek. I fall backward into the trunk space, stunned.

His twin goon steps up next to him, carrying a big roll of gray duct tape.

"This'll shut her up till we get there," he says, his tone

annoyed.

Oh no. Duct tape means rape. Death. No escape. The thoughts roll around my brain in a loop, and I begin to thrash and punch, heedless of the gun, but it's no use.

One holds me down while the other tapes up my mouth. Then they flip me over onto my stomach and smoosh my face into the carpeted base of the trunk, while the other drags my arms behind my back and lashes my wrists tightly together with the tape. They do the same to my ankles.

"We should teach the bitch a real lesson. Fucking cunt bloodied my nose." A rough hand shoves between my legs from behind, fingers poking and prodding, and I whimper into the carpet.

Not that. Please, not that.

Then the other one says, "Boss wants her intact. You willing to risk his rage by sampling the goods ahead of time?"

The hand is promptly removed, and even though I hate the "boss," whoever he may be, a little part of me is thankful for his intervention.

Even in absentia, his goons are obviously scared of him.

Then the lid slams shut, leaving me in darkness, and the car takes off again. I roll around among God knows what debris while I listen to the smooth purr of the car engine and hang on to my sanity by a thread.

Hot tears sprout and fall, unchecked, down my cheeks. My nose starts to drip uncontrollably, too, and numbly, I wonder if I'll suffocate before their "boss" gets the chance to rape and kill me.

Try not to think about your friends, who may or may not be dead.

Try not to hyperventilate.

Try to stay alive.

2

Rio

THE RED WELT across her left cheek stands out, because the rest of her face is so pale. Is she about to faint? Not that it will have much impact if she does, because she's already lying on the floor of the guest suite, trussed up like a Christmas turkey.

Her long dark hair spills every which way, and her glare above the duct tape covering half her face could probably bore a hole through metal.

Those eyes, almost golden in this moment, are like trea-cle, with a darker hue around the edge of the irises that gives her a seductive air. The photograph in the file did not do them justice.

Slowly, I turn to my second. "*You* brought her here and left her like this? Who hit her?"

He swallows, staring down at the Carlotti woman with a slight frown. "No, sir... Boss, I mean... No. Two Delta team members brought her in. This is the first I've seen of the situation."

"I gave explicit orders not to touch her. That will be my prerogative, if and when I choose."

"Yes, sir."

"What do you intend to do about it, Danelli?"

"Talk to the team. Find out who touched her, and deal with it."

"Ensure you do. And then consider how my orders, and the actions that ensued, did not match. I will not tolerate that situation again. This is your first—and *only*—warning. Out."

My second scurries from the room, closing the door behind him with a soft click.

Danelli makes a good second. That's the only reason I cut him slack in this instance. I will consider how to punish him later.

I turn my attention to the woman on the floor. Even now, with her tearstained and snot-covered face, she is glaring at me as if she wants to kill me.

A smile threatens to lift my lips. Perhaps the Mafia princess is buried somewhere deep inside her, after all.

I squat down in front of her. "I am going to remove the tape, and you will remain quiet and not fight me. If you do, I will call my second back in, and tell him to put a bullet between those beautiful golden-brown eyes of yours. Understand?"

The eyes in question widen briefly, and she nods.

There is no easy way to remove duct tape. I rip the gray material from her wrists first, then her ankles, leaving her face until last.

"Ready, Bianca?"

She sits up, rubbing her red-marked wrists. After a moment, another stiff nod gives me my answer. I rip away the tape. The second I do, she scurries backward across the floor in a crab-like move until her back hits the edge of the sofa.

She swipes a hand over her face, attempting to clean herself up, before she speaks. "I don't know who you are, but my name is not Bianca. You have the wrong person."

Her voice is low and raspy. She wasn't bound long enough to become dehydrated, so the hoarse effect must be from stress.

I stand and tilt my head, studying her. That welt across her face is starting to swell. Fear is evident in her taut features and the way she folds her arms across her middle, and yet she raises her chin and stares back at me with a defiant expression.

There are not many who would meet my gaze so boldly.

"I am Gregorio Agosti."

The simple sentence has the desired effect. Her lips part slightly before she drops her gaze.

Good. That recognition means I don't need to explain the danger she's in if she doesn't do what she's told.

"You're... I know that name. From the news. They call you Rio."

"Indeed." There have been many news stories about my organization, and about me.

Most, these days, are positive, focusing more on my

11

donations to charity than other things. I have learnt over the years that money can buy anything. Including legitimacy.

She moistens her lips with the tip of her tongue. I am not sure what about the action catches and holds my attention.

"Did…did your men…kill my friends?" There's a tremor on that last whispered word, and her brows come together in a frown.

Clearly, she does not like showing weakness.

My inner monster rears its ugly head. I will enjoy breaking this one in.

"No idea. I do not concern myself with collateral damage, Bianca."

"*Collateral…*" She sucks in a breath before her knees draw up and she wraps her arms around them.

She looks like a broken little bird.

Something stirs in the emptiness deep within me.

Something that disappears quickly when she sits up straight and speaks in a stronger voice. "It's Bree. Bree Walker. I'm *not* Bianca."

Suddenly, I am bored with the conversation. I move to the door of the suite. "Bree Walker is dead. You were born Bianca Carlotti, and from now on, that is the name you will answer to."

"Like hell." Her mutter is almost not there at all.

I am not sure if she meant for me to hear it.

I don't bother admonishing her. We both know she will do exactly as I say, in the end.

"There is a bathroom through there." I point across the room. "Shower. Clean yourself up. Someone will be back with a change of clothing for you, and some ice for that welt on your face. One hour, Bianca. That's how much time you have before I return."

I close and lock the door, and when I hear the sobs begin on the other side, my inner monster begins to purr.

———

Bree/Bianca

HE'S A MONSTER. Attractive. Intriguing. But at his core, emotionless and depraved.

Those news stories about him may skirt around the truth, but everyone in Boston knows Rio Agosti runs his Mafia crew with an iron fist and no ounce of compassion in his soul.

Does he even *have* a soul?

The whole *city* fears the reach of the Agosti-Carlotti cartel and its terrifying boss.

Including me, even though I've never had any involvement in crime of any description, let alone the organized variety.

You were born Bianca Carlotti.

Goose bumps rise up on my skin at the memory of those words. It was all I could do not to burst into tears and beg for my life at his feet.

But I saw it in his eyes—the sudden desire for me to do exactly that. It was the only hint of emotion I saw in him at all.

I will not give that man the satisfaction of begging. Not for anything.

I have no idea if Dave and Shelley are alive or dead. I have no idea why the Mafia monster's henchmen grabbed me. Clearly, it must be a case of mistaken identity. How can I convince him of that?

What if I can't?

Nausea rises, and I stumble up and into the bathroom. Even as I locate the toilet and heave up the meager contents of my stomach, my brain whirs at my surroundings. This damn bathroom is nearly as big as my apartment.

And... Briefly, I turn my head. Is that a gold bathtub? Surely it can't be *real* gold?

What sort of people live like this? Luxury and violence, side by side.

I heave again, until there is nothing left to bring up, and then I hug the bowl as I sob.

If I want to survive, I have to stop this pitiful crying and try to figure out how to escape.

Easier said than done.

I stand, and when I catch sight of my reflection in the intricately framed mirror, I recoil. *God.* I'm covered in flecks of blood and remnants of vomit, and there are wet splotches on my T-shirt where tears haven't yet dried. My left cheek is swollen, starting to purple. I lean in and poke at the area gently, wincing at the pain.

Did that goon break my cheekbone? I hope I broke his nose with my kick.

I need to shower, not only because I'm filthy, but because my brain won't stop imagining what may happen if I don't do as he says. If I behave, maybe he'll let me go.

Yeah, right. Because he seems like a decent guy who'll take pity on me, for sure.

I ignore my inner voice and take a couple of minutes to explore the rest of the suite, checking the door first even though I heard the decisive snick of the lock when he left.

There doesn't seem to be any other way out. There are windows in the bathroom, bedroom, and sitting room—the latter featuring huge floor-to-ceiling panes of glass that I'm sure are spectacular when sunlight filters through—but none of them open. Even if they did open, there is no balcony or even a fire escape outside. Only a fall several stories down to the concrete pavement below.

We must be in the city, judging by the view of other buildings outside, none of which contain any sign of people who may be able to call the cops. We are likely above a club of some kind, I'd guess, given the muted thrum of music rising up through the floor.

Is this *his* building? Does he run a slew of clubs, along with all his other business activities?

Figures. I *hate* clubs.

Panic threatens, and I curl my toes in the thick white carpet beneath my feet, trying to ground myself. He probably won't kill me here. I mean, who would want to spoil the pristine whiteness of this décor?

Textured wallpaper on the walls, patterned again in white with gold and silver overtones, provides a luxurious if slightly overdone feel, while the electric fireplace is flanked by white leather sofas and topped by a grand marble mantel that matches the marble featured in the bathroom.

In the next room is the biggest bed I've ever seen—surely it must be custom-made? I stare at that bed, wondering if other women before me were held here. If anything happened to them...in that bed...beneath his firm, unrelenting hands and body...

And that dead, emotionless gaze.

I shudder, tucking dangerous thoughts away.

Everything in this place points to luxury and decadence.

A luxurious gilded cage.

And I'm the poor canary trapped by the monster, for a purpose yet to be determined.

A glance at the clock above the fireplace reveals that some time has passed since he left. My heart thumps wildly before settling, and I scurry into the bathroom and shower as quickly as I can. Afterward, I towel dry my hair and dress in a fluffy white robe that was hanging on the back of the door.

I can't bring myself to put my vomit-stained clothes back on. Instead, I stuff them into a hamper in a corner of the room, wondering if I'll ever see them again.

Then I head out to the sitting area and wait, trying to slow-breathe so I can remain calm, until the snick of the door lock causes me to jump. My already edgy system kicks straight back into overdrive.

It isn't *him*. The monster. Instead, a gray-haired, older woman enters, holding a garment bag over one arm, a pair of spiky black heels in one hand, and an ice pack in the other.

From the way she's dressed, in a traditional-style black-and-white uniform, I assume she must be a housekeeper. Though, if this is a club in a city building, then "housekeeping" is a relatively loose term.

"Hello, dear," she says, a half-smile on her face.

"Please." I jump to my feet, rush over, and grab her by the arm. "Can you help me? I need to get out of here. Please, I need—"

"*Enough.*" Her tone is instantly frosty, and the pleasant expression disappears. "Get dressed. And fix your hair; it's a mess. Then put this on your cheek."

She hands me the ice pack.

"I will return in twenty minutes to help you disguise *that*." She points to my swollen face. "Be ready."

She drapes the garment bag over the back of the sofa, leaves the shoes, and departs the suite. I wait for the snick of the lock.

16

And wait.

And wait some more.

Eventually I creep over to the door and try the handle, a rush of dizziness almost flooring me when it opens.

Oh my fucking God. She didn't lock me back in.

I poke out my head, glancing left and right, but the corridor is empty. An elevator directly across from where I'm standing displays lit numbers above, showing that the car is descending.

Holy hell.

Thoughts leave my head, and I run.

Down the hallway in my robe and bare feet, aiming for the door at the end marked Fire Stairs. I slither to a stop, my heart pounding so hard I can barely hear anything else.

What will happen if I do this? If I defy a Mafia crime lord and make a run for it? How far will I get before he finds me? Before he…punishes me?

A frisson of something too dark to admit shivers across my skin.

Get out, I tell myself. *Now.*

I push open the fire door and rush through, only to collide with a hard male body and bounce back into the doorframe, cracking the back of my head. I groan at the pain and stare up.

And up.

Straight into Rio Agosti's coldly furious expression.

3

"All things truly wicked start from innocence."
Ernest Hemingway

Rio

THE TERROR in her expression is the only thing that saves her from my wrath.

When she collapses against my chest, looking up at me in that way, as if I'm the monster under the bed who has come to kill her, my cock hardens instantly, and thoughts of killing her recede.

Her hands scrabble ineffectually at my silk shirt, and a tiny moan escapes her lips.

Instead of reaching for my gun, holstered discreetly beneath my suit jacket, I grab her wrists. She is so delicately built that I can get the fingers of one hand around both of them.

I step forward, the action forcing her through the fire door into the corridor, and then I swivel to the side until her back is against the wall. I drop her wrists, pinning her in place by planting one arm on each side of her head.

"Going somewhere, Bianca?"

"I…" She licks her lips, her gaze dropping down toward the floor.

The thick white robe, like her shapeless clothing earlier, hides her body, though the dip at its neckline allows an enticing glimpse of lightly curving flesh beneath. I wonder what she'd do if I ripped the robe down off her shoulders and allowed it to pool at her waist.

My hands curl into fists beside her head as my need rises. I *want* to expose her, to teach her that it is not acceptable to defy me.

I lean in, so close our breaths mingle. Her scent rises around me, light and citrusy. "There is no escape, little bird. You will leave here when I say so, and not before."

Her eyelids flutter, her gaze remaining mostly downcast, allowing a view of tiny blue veins across her lids, like a network beneath her porcelain skin.

"I'm sorry," she whispers, but there is a note in her voice that doesn't quite ring true.

"Are you?"

Her eyes flash open then, staring straight into mine. I have to fight the urge to draw back from the shock of their amber depths so close.

Something flares in her expression that the predator in me recognizes but cannot name. I could kiss her, right now, and every instinct I possess says she would not push me away.

She fears me. And she wants me. And she hates both of those things.

"I *am* sorry," she says.

I study her, debating within myself whether or not she's worth keeping around.

She is likely pretending docility to keep me on side, but I know the truth. She is still considering how to escape. And yet, that terror-filled gaze as she rushed through the fire door was not feigned.

Her fear feeds the desire within me in a way I haven't experienced in a long time.

The monster under the bed has nothing on me.

I step back and gesture toward the suite she has just left. Wordlessly, she shifts off the wall and trudges back down the hallway.

As she reaches the door, she turns back to look at me. "Your men snatched me off the street and shot my friends. They bound me. *Hit* me. Did you really expect me *not* to try and run?"

"The man who hurt you will likely already be dead." I hope the pronouncement gives her comfort.

Why I want to offer that to her is not something I wish to dwell on.

"Dead? You mean, like Dave and Shelley? My friends. Is that your solution to everything? Shoot and kill. And your problems just…disappear?"

She doesn't sound comforted.

I draw my brows together. "Yes."

Laughter slips out of her; only, the sound is wrong. Not joyful, but hovering on the edge of hysteria.

"I am not in the habit of killing innocent people, Bianca."

She opens and closes her mouth a couple of times. "And yet, my friends *were* innocent."

Her voice is a whisper, almost not there at all.

I resist the urge to say more on the matter, instead pulling out my phone and punching in a number. I do not need to justify myself to anyone, let alone a Carlotti.

"Get dressed. You have five minutes, or I come in there and dress you myself, and if I have to do that, you will not like it." I raise the phone to my ear and turn away from her in dismissal.

Bree/Bianca

THE DRESS IS BLACK. Long and sleek and figure-hugging, with tiny spaghetti straps that probably won't do much to hold up my cleavage, even though I'm relatively flat-chested.

The organized crime lords like their women beautiful and sexy and dressed up, or so the media would have us all believe. Trophy women, on the arms of their powerful men.

This dress will qualify, but I'm sure my swollen cheek won't fit in with the look. Especially without makeup to cover the bruising.

Five minutes doesn't give me time to do anything more than rush into the bathroom, run a brush through my hair to tidy up, and then clasp it back at the nape of my neck with a jeweled clip I find in the top drawer of the cabinet. If those are real diamonds, then I've probably got more dollar value sitting in my hair right now than the average house.

I then race back out to unzip the garment bag and don the set of lacy black underwear I find inside before pulling on the dress.

Creepily, it all fits perfectly, even the set of heels for my larger-than-average feet. Almost like they knew I was coming and prepared everything beforehand.

There was a look in Rio's eye that said I'd pushed him too far out in the hallway, and I don't want to risk punishment if I disobey him yet again.

The man who hurt you will likely already be dead.

My hands tremble so hard I can't zip up the damn dress. I wish the housekeeper had come back, but Rio probably dismissed her for the night.

Five minutes to the second after I reentered the suite—I know because I'm watching the clock above a small desk in the corner of the lounge area—he opens the door and strides in.

I turn my back to him, silently requesting his assistance with the zipper.

Moments later, the touch of his fingertips on the skin of my lower back, where the zipper starts, sends tendrils of warmth through me. A shiver rushes up my spine from the connection.

My mouth tightens. He's a monster. His touch shouldn't have any effect on me except revulsion.

"Come," is all he says, when my dress is fastened and I turn back to face him.

There is no emotion in his expression. *Nothing* is readable in his eyes.

He leads the way out, this time to the elevator, where he punches the button without comment.

It isn't until we are in the car, descending, that he deigns to look at me via our reflections in the mirrors lining the walls. "I made a call. Your friends are alive."

Alive? Dave and Shelley aren't dead?

"Oh, my God." I didn't realize how much I was holding

in until this moment. I sag back against the wall of the car, tears pricking at my eyes. "I thought... I mean, I heard your guy *shoot* them."

"Hospital. One will likely walk with a limp. The other..." He shrugs.

What does that shrug mean? My throat hurts so badly I can barely swallow. I blink a few times, trying to remain in control.

I do not want to break down in front of this man. I suspect he would enjoy that.

"Okay," I manage after a few seconds, and when my legs don't collapse beneath me and I don't throw up the bile left in my stomach, I decide I've never been prouder of myself.

A grunt is his only response. Then the elevator doors ping open, and the music that had been a background thrum upstairs blares loudly, the blast of sound rushing in to envelop the space and take my breath away.

Last time I was at a club, I was drugged and almost assaulted by a guy who offered to buy me a drink. It wasn't this club, but the look, the feel, the sounds and smells, are all similar.

Luxury on the surface, a veneer of respectability, and underneath, sex and drugs and violent crime just waiting for an opportunity to burst free.

I begin to laugh, almost uncontrollably, only stopping when Rio lays a hand on the small of my back and pushes me forward, out of the elevator.

Several suited men are waiting as we exit, and they fall into step around us as Rio guides me along a raised walkway above the dance floor one level below. The floor is teeming with undulating bodies. A DJ works a bank of equipment on a raised dais at one end, while busy waitstaff deliver trays of drinks to waiting patrons seated at tables around the edges of the room.

The end of the walkway widens out into what appears to be a VIP-style viewing area, containing luxurious-looking couches and conversation pits, with a more refined-looking bar stretching across the back of the space, behind which several extremely attractive staff are mixing and serving drinks.

I take a seat where Rio points, on a couch right in the center of the viewing area, up front near the glassed-in barrier; the perfect vantage point to look out over the club.

"This is your place?" I slant a look his way, once he has finished murmuring in the ear of a thickset guy who is not hiding the fact that he is carrying a weapon.

That guy, and three others, stands nearby, watchful but not intrusive.

Rio sits beside me. Too close. Why does he not sit opposite?

"The building is mine, and this club. This whole city block is mine, Bianca. So, if you run, you will not get far. Remember that."

Drinks appear in front of us as if by magic. A heavily made-up blonde hands me a fluted glass full of bubbly alcohol off the tray in her hands. I glance at Rio who waits, as if expecting me to take a sip.

I place the drink back on the tray. "I don't want a drink. I don't want to be here at all. And my name is not Bianca. It's *Bree*. I told you—"

"And *I* told *you* to behave." Despite the music and the voices rising up from below, his tone is commanding.

It rubs me precisely the wrong way.

"What will you do if I don't? Kill me in front of all these

people…" What can he do with this many witnesses? Surely, if I simply stand up and walk out of here…

A shocked gasp from the waitress precedes a crash as she drops the tray. Glasses shatter. Her eyes are round and wide and full of horror as she falls to her knees amongst the debris, apologizing profusely.

I can't tell if her horror is because of her own mishap, or because of what I said.

Rio ignores her, as if she's not even there. Ignores the other staff who rush over to help her clear up the mess.

Instead, he leans so close to me, his breath brushes over my cheek and ear when he speaks. "If you do not behave, Bianca, I will bend you over this railing, lift up your dress, and give you the spanking you so clearly crave."

4

"A caged bird stands on the grave of dreams..."
Maya Angelou

Bree/Bianca

His words strike where I least expect, with a rush of heat right between my legs.

Oh, God. No.

I don't want to feel anything positive for this monster.

I'm still trying to process my reaction when he says, "And not a single one of these people, my dear"—he splays out a hand to indicate everyone in the vicinity—"will lift a finger to help you. Because, unlike you, they know the consequences if they do."

I should be horrified at his words, at my response. I *am* horrified.

Would he really spank me in front of everyone, right here

in the club? Why is my body intent on betraying me at that thought? I don't understand what is happening to me.

I can't breathe. He's too close.

I jump to my feet and shuffle around the low table in front of us, putting welcome space between me and him. I'm right at the railing now—the railing he just threatened to bend me over—and I turn away from his unreadable regard and grip the silver metal so hard I wonder if I may accidentally put dents in it.

I feel like I've died and woken up in a strange kind of hell.

Who lives like this, with the threat of violence and death tainting every breath, every action? Who thinks it okay to kidnap an ordinary person off the street, shoot their friends, and then expect them to sit and calmly drink in a club only a few hours later, surrounded by people who carry guns?

But worse than all of that…what sort of sick woman feels the lick of desire heat her privates at the thought of being spanked by her kidnapper, in front of a crowd of strangers?

Everyone down below is oblivious to what is going on up here.

If I scream at the top of my lungs, will anyone hear me? Will anyone actually care?

I hover on the verge of trying it out, until I feel him close behind me. I don't even have to look to know it's him. His scent—some kind of spicy aftershave more subtle than I expect from a crime lord—wafts into my nostrils.

I *hate* that he smells good.

He should smell like death.

"Why am I here, Gregorio?"

"You called me Rio earlier."

I don't want to turn and face him. I *can't* face him. Not

27

yet. Not while thoughts of being spanked keep swirling in my head.

I stare down at the ignorant crowd. "I don't know *what* to call you."

"Rio will suffice."

"Fine. Rio. Please answer my query."

He sighs and moves to stand beside me. I shoot a glance his way, relieved that he seems to be focused on the crowd instead of me.

"You are here because I am about to have a business meeting I can't delay, and because I need you with me when the results of your DNA testing come in."

"My...*what*?" Now I do turn to face him. "When did you... How..."

He tilts his head toward me and smirks. His eyes remain dark and unreadable, but his lips lift as if he's finally enjoying himself.

"My team have a rapid DNA system in place. They are processing the duct tape we removed from you earlier, together with strands of your hair. The results are imminent, and when they come in, we will confirm your identity against the DNA from your last remaining cousin who died last month in prison."

There are so many shocking aspects to that statement, I don't know where to start with it.

If I thought I was having trouble breathing earlier, now it is as if all the air in the whole building just got sucked right out.

"I...ah..." Putting aside the fact that rapid DNA testing is supposed to be only available to organizations like the FBI... "So, you're not certain that I'm her? Bianca? If the results don't match, will you let me go?"

"I am certain. We have already tested your DNA once. This second test is just to confirm. Your real family allowed your nanny to take you and run when you were only six months old. Right before most of your family was wiped out, Bianca."

The taunting words whisper over me, and I want to sob. Wiped out? Does he mean murdered?

"The trail was lost when the nanny placed you into the adoption system. For a time, at least. But we found the nanny, followed the trail, and here you are."

Yes, I was adopted, but so were thousands of others. Millions of others, probably.

Why does he assume I'm a Carlotti—and the only surviving one, from the sounds of it?

My adoptive parents told me what happened to my birth family, and it didn't involve anything remotely Mafia or cartel-related—my birth parents died when a drunk truck driver plowed into their car, and when my only remaining relative, an elderly great-aunt, passed away the same month from cancer, I was put into the system and eventually adopted out. I have no cousins that I'm aware of. Certainly none who spent time in prison.

The DNA results won't match; I'm certain of it. What I'm not so sure about is whether this crazy mob guy will actually let me go. He seems to be fixated on me being Bianca Carlotti, who I'm guessing is someone who could challenge his power base, given he's the nominal head of the Agosti-Carlotti cartel.

A tiny piece of the jigsaw falls into place.

He needs to maintain his position, and he's worried I may threaten that.

The situation would be laughable, if it weren't so terrifying. I can't believe it is happening, and I don't know how to make it stop.

He has the wrong girl. I'm not a Carlotti. Not in a million years.

Rio

SHE HAS the look of a frozen deer in headlights, but I cannot take more time to explain or coddle her. Danelli has appeared in the VIP area, which means Anders has arrived downstairs.

I had hoped for the phone call about the DNA results before now, but no matter. I will take care of business with Anders, and then focus back on the Carlotti girl afterward.

I nod at my second. *I am ready. Send him up.*

I turn to Bianca. "Wait at the bar until I'm done."

She does not need to overhear this conversation, though she needs to be visible. As soon as the DNA results confirm things, I will let her know what I really need from her, beyond being bait for Anders's boss.

This time round, she doesn't argue, but instead scurries across the room and slides onto a barstool in the farthest corner of the space. Good. Exactly where I want her, though it is obvious she is trying to get as far away from me as she can.

Too bad for her there are no dark corners where my influence doesn't reach in this city.

I catch Danelli's eye yet again and jerk my chin in Bianca's direction, silently telling him to keep an eye on her. After a moment's hesitation, in which he follows my gaze, he moves closer to where she's seated, but his eyes are curious when he stares back at me. I don't want to know what that look is about.

Then the elevator pings, and Anders is here.

Time to forget anything personal and focus only on the matter at hand. The possible betrayal of my crew—my family —by Anders's boss, Rossi.

The traitor's man and his two companions have been patted down prior to being allowed up. They know it is a condition of meeting with me that their weapons are left at the door.

Equally, I know at least one of the three, if not all of them, may still have a weapon hidden somewhere on their person that my men did not catch. I would do the same if I were in their shoes. Never voluntarily surrender all your weapons. Survival of the fittest 101.

I take a seat on the couch vacated by the Carlotti girl, and gesture for Anders to join me.

His gaze is everywhere, assessing and calculating, before he takes a seat on the couch opposite mine. I would not expect anything less than the vigilance he displays. If Anders did not work for Rossi, I would likely offer him a position on my crew.

His henchmen make a move to join him, but two of my men step forward, holding them back.

Anders waves a hand, letting them know to stay where they are, near the bar. As if it is his choice, and not mine, as to how this meeting will play out.

I raise a brow and wait for him to start.

"You're a hard one to catch up with, Rio," he says. "Rossi sends his regards and his thanks for agreeing to see me tonight, after…you know…"

He smiles with a fake-friendly air that fools no one. He

likely saw the hand of Rossi's henchman, fingers still clutching the gun, that my crew sent back to Rossi in a box after the failed assassination attempt.

I was kind. I even returned the bullets, albeit in a second box.

I sit forward, resting my hands on my knees, and stare at him with the look I know some have described as a vision of imminent death.

His Adam's apple bobs as he swallows, and his smile fades away to nothing.

"I agreed to meet with you, Anders, because I have a message for your boss and I need you to deliver it in person."

Casually, I draw my gun from the holster at my side and lay the barrel across one knee.

"Fuck, Rio. I didn't come here to make trouble—"

"Tell Rossi I have the Carlotti girl," I cut in.

Anders's head jerks up, and his mouth drops open before he swivels to reassess the room.

His gaze lands on Bianca, sitting alone at the bar with a watchful Danelli hovering nearby, her long legs crossed in an elegant fashion. One high-heeled foot twitches in a small sign of nerves. A cascade of dark hair tumbles down her back, secured at the nape of her neck by a sparkling clip.

The swollen cheek and eye are not visible from this angle, and she looks every inch the assured Mafia princess as she stares down into her drink, twirling the contents aimlessly with a straw.

Something unfamiliar stirs inside me. I tamp it back down. I need to concentrate on the matter at hand.

Anders returns his gaze to me. "Her? Holy shit, man, are you sure? Everyone's been looking for her for years."

"And *I* found her." I glance at my Rolex. No need to let

him know I am yet to receive the DNA confirmation. "We will be married within the week, and the Agosti-Carlotti union will be official and irrevocable. The cartel will be mine. Tell your boss that if he wishes to keep doing business in this state, he had better back down now. He has lost, but there is opportunity for both of us, if he toes the line."

"*Your* line, you mean? He won't like that."

Anders is pale, my message clear, but he needs to posture a little to save face. I can't be bothered with it. Anders's ego is Carlos's problem, not mine.

"Yes. My line. And I don't care if Carlos likes it or not. You may leave." I nod at Danelli, and several of my men step forward to ensure the three visitors are escorted out.

When they're gone, I lean back, satisfied. No bloodshed required, at least for tonight.

Putting Bianca over by the bar was not only to stop her from hearing our discussion. It was to give her somewhere to shelter, should Anders or his men decide they preferred to shoot first and ask questions later.

My phone pings at that moment with the message I've been waiting for.

I read the text and open the report that accompanies it before looking at Bianca. She is glaring at me with a stormy gaze that morphs into confusion, and then outright fear, as she glances down at the phone in my hand and back up to meet my eyes.

I smile, a predator with his prey.

Bianca Carlotti is about to get the shock of her life when I show her these results.

Time to set the Agosti-Carlotti cartel permanently in place, and get this cursed marriage game underway.

5

"Nearly all men can stand adversity, but if you want to test a man's character, give him power."
Abraham Lincoln

Bianca

I STARE DOWN at the DNA results confirming I am Bianca Carlotti, last remaining heir of the Carlotti crime family.

"Uh-uh. No way." I shake my head.

Only once I start, I don't seem able to stop. I shake and shake until Rio reaches out and grabs my chin to stop the movement.

"You are her. I already knew it in here." He taps his chest with a fist. "These results confirm it."

"They're fake. I don't believe you."

Nausea roils in my stomach. I seem to be making a habit of throwing up since I fell into this nightmare earlier today.

Good thing I've had nothing to eat for hours and there's fuck all left in my stomach to bring up.

"I don't care if you believe me or not. I needed to know, and now I do. So, this is how it is going to play out, Bianca."

I open and close my mouth. Claiming that I'm Bree Walker seems moot at this point. No one believes it here, other than me. And these results...

I stare again at the report. This isn't a fly-by-night outfit that made something up. This report comes from one of the most prestigious medical facilities in Boston.

Unless the letterhead is fabricated, too.

Were my birth parents actual Mafia? I can't imagine it. The whole concept is so far removed from the life I've always known that it seems like a ludicrous idea.

I look up into Rio's eyes, and for the first time, I see something other than emptiness. He's excited by this news in a way that scares me even more.

Scares me, and excites me. And I don't want to feel *anything* along those lines.

"When you say this is going to play out... Um, do I get to go home at some point?"

Even as I ask the question, I know the answer is going to be one I don't want to hear.

He looks almost pitying before his lips lift slightly at the corners.

"You *are* home. This is your life now. You should start to get your head around that, because it is not going to change."

"Living above a club, locked in the suite upstairs, for what purpose?"

I don't know why I keep pushing, goading him. His reputation may be legit in the media these days, but the dark stories of the past remain. Gregorio Agosti is not someone to antagonize. Not in any way, shape, or form. Those who do tend to end up "disappeared."

And I don't want to disappear. I've only just turned twenty-five. I *like* life.

"Not here. I will move you to my family estate in the morning, and then, eventually, we will be married."

"Okay." I don't mean, *okay, I agree*. My brain simply stops working, and I have nothing left but numbness.

Okay in this instance means, *I literally have no idea how to think, feel, or respond to what you've just said, you psychopathic monster.*

My silence doesn't seem to faze him. "That's how this is going to play out, Bianca. You will become my wife, and I will gain control of the Carlotti cartel once and for all. Legally. Because you will sign it over to your new husband as a wedding gift."

After he dismisses me and one of his men returns me to the suite upstairs, his words play over and over in my head.

The woman who brought the clothing earlier returns at some point with more clothing and a tray of food. I'm sitting on the couch, curled up in the corner hugging my legs, when the door clicks open and she walks in.

"You need to eat, young lady."

I stare down at my red-painted toenails. I painted them this morning before work… *Yesterday* morning, I correct, glancing at the clock above the desk and realizing it is after 2:00 a.m. I thought then, when I added the red glossy color to the tips of my toes, that it was fun to add a bit of glitz for my birthday—an occasion to be spent with my friends.

Not imprisoned here by a sexy maniac who insists I'm the long-lost child of a cartel he is obviously intending to control via marriage.

I clench my hands against my legs. "Thank you, but I'm not hungry."

"No. You will eat." She plonks the tray down on the coffee table and slides the whole table closer to me, grunting as she does so. "I will stay until you are done."

She folds her arms, looking resolute.

Holy hell, is this nightmare ever going to end?

I sit up properly and study the tray. At least the sandwich snack is light—given the hour, I don't want to try and force a big meal. I'm a morning person. I'm usually up and eating breakfast only a few hours from now.

What *is* normal anymore? A little voice in my head pipes up—the one that always leads me down the wrong garden path when I listen to it.

What if he's actually telling the truth?

Surely not.

I mean, I've heard of the Carlotti family, of course, and what happened to them. I think there may even have been a television miniseries made at one point. Anyone who grew up in this city knows at least something of the crime lord families who run things from the shadows.

But there's nothing in my history to hint that I'm the one who got away. The baby who, it was rumored, was either thrown into the river and drowned, or spirited away by the nanny before the rest of the family was murdered at a dinner party. It all depended on who was telling the story as to what was said.

I always liked the idea of the baby being rescued. That version speaks to my own start in life.

So, it's possible, the inner voice goads.

I was six months old when I was handed in to a church-run adoption agency in South Boston.

Sickness fills my gut, yet again, but this time I ignore it and shove pieces of peanut butter sandwich into my mouth, feeling wilful enough to glare at the older woman while I do so.

She rolls her eyes and her mouth thins, but at least she remains quiet until I finish.

I don't want to admit that I feel less nauseous once I've eaten. Instead, I just grab the mug of tea off the tray and cup my hands around its welcome warmth, turning away to stare toward the fake flames in the fireplace so I don't have to see her judgmental face anymore.

A few minutes later, she departs, and I release a sigh of relief.

If only the rest of this situation was so easily resolved.

Problem is, with Rio and the people he surrounds himself with, my death may be the only way out of this completely fucked-up scenario.

Rio

I ALMOST MANAGE to convince myself that I'm checking in on Bianca because she is valuable merchandise.

But there's no need for me to do this. I have staff for menial jobs, and a check-in on Bianca should be menial.

There is something about her that draws me in though. Something I don't wish to name.

She has changed into the pajama set that was left out for her while we were down in the club. An ivory-colored night-gown that finishes just above the knees, with some kind of over jacket that does nothing to hide the jut of her nipples beneath the satin fabric.

I rake my gaze over her body, and I'm not sure she even realizes that her protective gesture of folding her arms across her middle actually highlights rather than disguises her delicate curves.

She's very slim, nothing like the generously curvaceous women I enjoy in my bed. There is nothing in her to warrant the curl of lust that runs through me; nothing to ignite interest to the point that I can't seem to keep away.

I force myself to consider her with an impartial view. At least she ate the snack I sent up. The housekeeper informed me of that a half hour ago.

But that seems to be the extent of her cooperation. Right now, her eyes breathe fire, and her whole body shakes as she faces me.

"I want to make it clear, Rio. I will never agree to marry you. Not for any reason. You're a monster." She sucks in a breath on that last word, as if afraid she has just gone too far.

With anyone else, it would have been.

I step in close, making sure she reads the truth in my expression. "I *am* a monster. You should never forget that."

I reach out to touch her cheek, tracing the delicate bone structure and wondering if she will ever be strong enough to live this life I have mapped out for her. She feels so warm and soft. I drop my hand from her fragile features and turn away. If I don't, I'm not sure what I may do.

"You will marry me."

"No." There's a note in her voice that I don't understand. Defiance, and something dark underlying it that I can't read.

I swivel back to face her.

She licks her lips, and her gaze drops to my own. The curl of lust in my groin flares into something far less subtle.

I advance toward her, and she backs away, and keeps backing up until she reaches the wall next to the bedroom door. I crowd in, planting one hand on each side of her head and splaying my fingers out on the wall.

Her dark hair falls softly around her face and down over her shoulders. Her breathing is frantic, her breasts lifting and falling against my silk shirt. Her lips are parted, and her gaze is still on my mouth, only inches from her own. Her sweet, citrusy perfume wafts up into my nostrils.

I close the remaining inches between us and brush my mouth against hers.

Soft, so soft, but the promise of something far less sweet is there in the tiny moan that releases from her throat. I shift one of my hands to grip her neck, keeping my hold light. Her pulse beats fast beneath my fingertips, and her head tilts back slightly, as if giving me permission for more.

The fragility I sensed in her is gone. Somehow, it has disappeared in the space of a few seconds.

"I hate you so much," she breathes against my mouth.

I smile, feeling cruel. "Good. You should."

I bite at her lower lip, not vicious enough to draw blood, but enough to elicit another tiny sound from Bianca.

I release her mouth, but we remain like that for a moment or two longer before I step back, dropping my hand away from her neck to allow her to slide out and away from me if she wishes.

She doesn't move. She simply leans there against the wall, looking at me, her hands curled into fists at her sides.

My heart skips a beat. That look in her eyes is not fearful or confused. It is dark and full of passion and rage. My cock swells, heavy and uncomfortable, and I almost release a groan at the difficulty in bringing my body back under control.

"Leave me, Rio," she says, her voice husky. "I need to sleep now."

Fuck. If anyone else ordered me to leave a room...

My fists clench, too, and I concentrate on breathing evenly, before deciding to allow her some leeway this one time. She doesn't yet know the rules of this world. But she will.

I turn and head for the door, intending to put her presence out of my head once I leave here.

"I meant what I said. You *will* marry me," I say when I reach the entrance.

My voice is soft, but she flinches.

I decide to add incentive. "If you do not, Bianca, I will ensure the animal shelter you worked for is shut down, and everyone who worked there never finds another job in this state. Ever. There are consequences for your actions, always. Do you understand, little bird?"

6

"We are never trapped unless we choose to be."
Anais Nin

Bianca

YOUR ACTIONS HAVE CONSEQUENCES. Rio's cruel tone reverberates through the suite long after he has left. *You will
marry me.*

I clench the silken bed cover as I relive that little scene.
Over my dead fucking body.

My dead fucking body that is throbbing with need after
that delicious, monstrous, almost kiss.

What is wrong with me?

I raise my fingers to my lips, still feeling his essence all
around me. On me. I can smell his subtle scent every time I
move. My bottom lip hurts where he bit it, but with an ache
that is more a reminder of the kiss than an actual hurt.

I've heard of Stockholm syndrome. Who hasn't? But that's not what this is. I *hate* Gregorio Agosti with a passion. The fact that my body desires him, regardless of his behavior, disgusts me.

I don't want to desire a monster.

I fall back against the pillows, thinking about every moment since his goons snatched me off the street.

Could he be telling the truth? If I assume for a moment he is, and I really am the missing Carlotti heir, does it matter? Will it make his behavior any more excusable, or change what I want out of this situation?

Hell no.

I want to go home to my own life, and have nothing to do with this crazy environment full of organized crime and mob muscle men who think they can rule their own little world with an iron fist and threats of violence and death.

It seems as if I don't have any choice but to go along with his plan. For now. But Rio doesn't know me as well as he thinks.

I may or may not have started life as Bianca Carlotti, but I damn sure don't plan to sit around and accept the role he wants me to play.

He can't watch me twenty-four seven, and the moment he slips up, I'm out of here. Straight to the Feds. He may light up my unwilling body with his damn annoying sexual charisma, but I don't care. I will see the monster jailed for whatever I can get him on.

And I will laugh when they take him away in handcuffs.

THEY COME for me at ten the following morning. I barely slept, except for a few hours near dawn. I've been up, showered, and dressed since eight, and when the housekeeper brought in a tray of breakfast soon after, I made sure to eat the lot. I need to keep up my strength if I want to get out of this alive.

He said I'd be taken to his family estate just outside the city. For some reason, I expect to see Rio in the black limousine when I'm escorted downstairs by two of his men, but there is no one inside, barring the driver up front behind tinted glass.

At first, my heart leaps when I realize I may have a chance to slip away at a traffic light stop, but then the two goons follow me in and take a seat opposite.

They stare at me with matching blank gazes, and I wonder how much he pays them and what kind of dirty work they do for him. Escorting me to Rio's family home must seem like a step down from...whatever it is Mafia muscle does on a daily basis.

"Thanks, guys. It's nice to ride *inside* the vehicle this time instead of in the trunk," I quip at one point, but there is no response, so I sink back against the leather seat and stare out the dark-tinted window.

The ride west and then south takes less than an hour. A check of the road signage indicates that we are somewhere near Dover when we finally turn off the road and pull up in front of the entrance to what I can only describe as some kind of compound. There's a high wall heading off in each direction, and the black wrought-iron gates are tall and firmly shut.

That is, until the driver speaks into an intercom system, and the gates slide open to allow us entry.

When I stare out of the rear window once we pass inside,

the gates have already closed. The walls hid a beautiful garden with a faint tropical feel. How do they keep it like this in the colder months? So green and lush and full of color? Maybe he's so rich they simply rip everything out and start again each season?

The upside is that every window in the grand home just up ahead must look out onto pure beauty. The downside? How the heck am I going to escape from this place?

The driveway curves up and around to a grand portico entrance. We glide to a halt in front of huge double doors that instantly open to reveal someone standing ready to greet us. Yet another housekeeper? She is flanked by two men in suits who look like what they must be. Hired muscle for security purposes.

Great.

One of my goons opens the door and climbs out of the limo, gesturing me to follow.

When I'm outside, I take a moment to straighten my dress and look around. I can't see anything except high walls in the distance beyond the garden. Eventually, I bring my gaze back to the woman waiting at the top of the short flight of steps.

"Come inside, Bianca. Your suite is ready for you. Gregorio will be back in time to join you for dinner, so you'll have the afternoon to acquaint yourself with your new home."

A headache presses in at my temples, and I work my jaw to stop from grinding my teeth together.

I cannot believe that this time yesterday, I was at my job at the shelter, bathing and de-fleaing one of the new feline arrivals and wondering if Dave would finally get up the nerve to ask me out on a date.

Dave. And Shelley. A sick feeling settles into my gut. Rio said they would be okay, but can I believe him?

I climb the front steps and enter the house without answering the woman, who in all honesty doesn't seem to expect a response. Perhaps he kidnaps women and brings them home on a regular basis?

Deep down, I know he doesn't. I'm not sure how I know, but I do.

Rio Agosti is all business, and bringing me here against my will, with the aim of marrying me, seems a ridiculously illogical—even emotional—response to a situation I'm not sure I fully understand.

How can he possibly expect to gain control of the Carlotti business empire simply by marrying me? Is that how Mafia business deals work? Two people marry, and then the man automatically gains control of the woman's empire, whether she wants to hand it over or not?

It sounds archaic, like something from medieval times in which women have no rights at all.

I shiver and wrap my arms around my middle.

That is exactly how it sounds, and somehow, I'm stuck in the middle of it in a nightmare I don't know how to get out of.

ONCE INSIDE, I stop and take stock of my surroundings. I am in a huge foyer entrance with black-and-white marble flooring and grand columns up to high ceilings, all of which scream money and grandeur. The furniture is ornate and not to my taste—all white leather and heavily carved wood—but its opulence suits the décor.

I don't get the chance to explore downstairs at this time. The housekeeper gestures toward a large curved staircase, above which hangs the largest chandelier I've ever seen. I crane my neck as I follow her up the staircase, looking at the sparkling light.

For all I know, that chandelier is made of diamonds rather than crystals. It seems to fit with Rio's need for ostentatious splendor to have such a thing especially made.

The security guys stay downstairs, and I'm grateful for that small reprieve. Those gun bulges in their jackets are intimidating, to say the least.

At the top of the stairs is a long, carpeted hallway. About halfway down, the woman stops at a set of double doors and unlocks one of them with a key she pulls from a pocket.

"This will be your suite, until Gregorio states otherwise," she says calmly.

"Okay." I speak for the first time since arriving. "Thank you."

I mean, it's not her fault her employer is a monster.

Her brows lift as if I've surprised her. "You're welcome," she says in a slightly warmer tone. "I must say, you are not what I was expecting when Gregorio explained the situation."

I'll bet I'm not. Had she imagined a perfect Mafia princess? Someone who could hang off Rio's arm like a compliant, sparkly possession, and remain quiet except when spoken to?

"Did he tell you his men shot my friends when he snatched me off the street?" Unexpectedly, my eyes well up, and I blink hard.

I've been trying to keep that memory tamped down as far as I can.

They're alive. Remember that.

Her mouth thins, and she ignores my question. "I'll let

47

you settle in and explore. Ring the bell above the fireplace when you're ready for lunch. It will be brought to you."

She points through the door to my rooms, then turns to leave.

"What's your name?" I ask quickly, wondering if she'll help me escape if I establish a personal connection.

"I am Francine," she says. Her gaze shutters. "Please don't try to leave, Bianca. There are more guards here than you can imagine, and I do not wish to see you hurt. My nephew would be most displeased if his future wife was damaged."

My nephew?

She strides off down the hall, leaving me gaping after her.

Okay, then. Cross Aunt Francine off the list of people who may be able to help me. I'm back down to one name on that list.

Myself.

Rio

"It is done, Gregorio. She is in." My aunt's tone is difficult to read, and I curse the meeting that kept me here in the city until late in the day.

I would have preferred to be at the estate in person to judge Francine's reaction to Bianca. She sounds…uncertain.

"Good. Any trouble?" I tap my fingertips against the wooden desktop, awaiting her response.

Why is my aunt uncertain? I think about how many times Bianca has popped into my mind since I left her last night.

Far more times than I want.

A scowl drops my brows. What is it about her that has such an effect on me? But then, perhaps it isn't me. Perhaps it's Bianca who has an unsettling effect on everyone she meets. Is that why my aunt sounds the way she does right now?

"There was no trouble, Gregorio. But she has an attitude. Not respectful toward you. And she does not seem to fully understand her situation. Are you certain she's the right..." Francine trails off, as if realizing her error in questioning me.

"It is her." My tone is cold to remind her that I would never make such a rookie mistake as to mis-identify the Carlotti heir. "And she wouldn't understand. Not yet. It has not been properly explained to her. A fact I intend to rectify this evening over dinner. Ensure everything is ready for my arrival."

I push the button to end the call, and then steeple my fingers as I consider how best to proceed.

Marriage to Bianca will be a business transaction, nothing more. And in business, I am known for my ruthless nature. That is what I need to focus on this evening.

Not the way her hair falls so softly down her back. Not the way her eyes switch between enticing innocence and passion-filled rage deep in their depths. Definitely not the light citrus scent that, even now, hours later, lingers in my nostrils.

I release a growl and turn to the liquor cabinet to pour myself a whiskey.

Focus.

Soon, I will possess the Carlotti princess, and the plan I have been working toward for more years than I care to remember will finally come to fruition.

49

_____

7

"Revenge is sweet and not fattening."
Alfred Hitchcock

Bianca

I SPEND the rest of the day exploring the suite assigned to me and trying to figure out how to escape.

The space comprises several expensively decorated rooms, all with large, floor-to-ceiling windows leading onto a long balcony. I venture out onto the balcony in the fresh afternoon air, and discover Rio's family estate backs onto river frontage, with views that would be breathtakingly beautiful were it not for the circumstances surrounding my arrival here.

There is a pathway that leads from the house down to a landing dock on the river. Presumably he has a boat—or several, for all I know—but there is nothing docked there at present.

I consider climbing over the railing and somehow shimmying down the wall, but realize the futility of that thought when I notice men with walkie-talkies in hand, obviously patrolling the grounds.

One of the men has a large dog on a lead, and he stops at one point and looks up toward me.

At first, I shrink back from his sunglasses-covered perusal, but then I control my nerves and move forward to grip the balcony railing and stare down at him.

I may be completely out of my depth, scared of being killed at any moment, and unsure how—or if—I will ever get out of this situation, but I'm damned if I'll show that fear to any of these goons.

So, I raise my chin and glare at him, and after several seconds, he and the dog move on until they are out of sight among the trees.

When evening falls, Francine appears at the door of my suite. "Rio expects you to dress for dinner. Be ready at seven thirty, Bianca."

After she leaves, I check the door, assuming it will be locked, but shocked to find it open. I step out into the hallway, my heart pounding as I remember what happened the last time I tried this at the club. Rio's chest was so very hard and unforgiving.

I creep silently down the carpeted hallway to the set of stairs I used this morning. I'm halfway down, holding my breath, when a man steps seemingly out of nowhere and studies me from the base of the staircase.

His hands are clasped calmly in front of him, and there is no particular animosity in his expression, but the message is clear. That way is closed off to me, as well.

Tears well, and I swallow hard as I head back to my

rooms, trying to keep my emotions in check. The tears tumble out anyway, scudding down my cheeks, and I rush into the bathroom and strip off, deciding to jump under a shower to hide my sobs from anyone who may be listening.

For all I know, my whole suite is rigged with microphones and cameras to watch my every move.

It's like I've been caught in a never-ending nightmare. I can't see any way to wake up and get back to reality.

I sit on the base of the shower, letting the hot water rush over my shoulders and back.

"I'm Bree," I whisper, over and over. "Bree Walker. Even if I was born Bianca, I'm not her anymore. And I don't want to marry a murderer."

At seven thirty on the dot, a knock on the door of my suite signals it is time for whatever Rio has planned next for me. My heart rate kicks into overdrive.

After studying the almost endless array of clothing options in the massive walk-in wardrobe—in fact, I can't even call it a wardrobe; it's a whole room—I choose a simple ivory-colored shift dress and some nude pumps.

He probably wants me dressed like some kind of vamp whore, but for someone more used to jeans and T-shirts, this is as dressy as I can bring myself to achieve for a man I loathe.

I dab some makeup over my cheek—the swelling has receded, but the bruising has surfaced more—and leave my hair loose, letting it swirl over my shoulders and down my back. It may help to screen some of my emotions if I can't contain myself during dinner.

Francine raises a brow and purses her lips when she sees me, but says nothing. She escorts me down the stairs and across the foyer area into a large dining space without a word being spoken between us. Clearly, I haven't passed muster with my choice of dress for the evening.

Too bad, Auntie.

Rio is already waiting in the room, standing by a marble-topped sideboard and pouring himself a drink. He looks like he's come straight from the office, in charcoal-colored suit trousers and a white dress shirt, though he is minus a tie and jacket.

There's a weariness to the line of his shoulders that I haven't noticed before, and yet when he turns and studies me, the weariness instantly disappears.

He studies me from head to toe and back again, but I can't read anything on his face other than his usual impassivity.

"Drink?" he says eventually, raising the decanter in his hand.

The liquid inside is ruby-red, and I assume it must be red wine, perhaps left out to breathe by some loyal staff member.

"Sure." I shrug, wondering how this evening will play out.

Will it be civilized on the surface, with a pretense that we are an ordinary betrothed couple besotted with one another and eager to plan our nuptials?

"Sit," Rio says, handing me a glass of wine and pointing to one of the set places at the table. "We will talk terms over dinner."

I guess civility is overrated in his world.

I want to remain standing, just to spite him, but what would be the point? I take a seat where he indicates, at one of two places set at a dining table that must seat possibly twenty people when it's full.

"So, this is your family's estate?" At his nod, I add, "Where is your family, then? I haven't seen anyone today except your aunt and security guys."

He moves to his place, directly opposite me, and takes his time sitting down. "I have two younger brothers, both of whom are away on family business at present. My sister is in her final year of boarding school and will be joining us when she graduates. She will live here until I secure her a suitable marriage. My aunt and her son Tommaso live here, too, though Tommaso is also away visiting family in Italy.

"That is all the family I have or need, Bianca. My role is to lead the business, and ensure its survival in this cutthroat world in which we live."

There is so much wrong in that short explanation that I'm not sure how to respond. His poor sister. An arranged marriage? I don't want to goad him too far, but there's a glaring omission in his explanation.

"And your parents?" I ask. "Where are…?"

He spears me with that terrifying look I've secretly dubbed his almost-dead expression, and I check out from finishing the sentence.

"Sorry," I say, ducking my head to take a quick sip of wine.

The alcohol does nothing to steady my nerves.

He doesn't answer. Instead, we sit in awkward silence until a server enters the room and dishes up our first course. It's soup, but I have no idea what kind other than to note that it is green. I'm too tense to identify the taste. The prospect of eating dinner across from this man is becoming more difficult by the second.

It is not until the server leaves the room that he tilts his head to one side and says in a conversational tone, "I have no parents, Bianca. They were killed a long time ago by one of my business rivals. You, little bird, are going to form part of my plan for revenge."

Rio

MANY THOUGHTS SWIRL in my head as dinner progresses. The one that bothers me most is the way my heart seemed to skip a beat when Bianca entered the dining room.

I don't allow anything in my life that threatens my self-control. Clearly, Bianca's presence does just that. And yet, I need her here to secure the Carlotti business in a legal fashion, and shore up the Agosti power base so that no one can take it away.

In that almost-white dress, with her hair tumbling down her back like a dark cascade, and so little makeup that I can see a smattering of freckles across the bridge of her nose as well as the purpling bruise on her cheekbone where Danelli's man hit her, she is nothing like the women in my world.

She is innocent and naïve, and if there were any other way to get what I need, I would cut her loose.

There is not.

If I don't use her, one of my rivals will. And they will be less lenient than I in how she is treated.

Bianca's innocence is only an asset in this world, until someone secures it for themselves.

I need to ensure that someone is me.

I wait until dessert and coffee are served before I speak on the matter.

"There is a meeting later tonight that I need you to be present for," I say.

She jumps in her chair, as if my very voice frightens her, but then her mouth sets in a stubborn line and she shoots me a look that says very clearly that she is not afraid of me. She gives off so many mixed messages, I cannot quite get a read on her.

"What sort of meeting, and why do you need me there, Rio?"

"A business meeting. I wish to introduce you as my fiancée, and I need you to cooperate with that concept."

"Hmm." She taps her lips with a finger, the action instantly drawing my attention to her mouth.

I want to ravish that mouth until it is swollen and begging me for more. And then I want it wrapped around my cock while I sink my fingers into her beautiful hair and guide her head while she pleasures me.

I shift in my chair, ignoring the desire that begins to harden my flesh. "I meant what I said earlier, Bianca. There will be dire consequences for those you care about, should you not comply with my wishes."

"Oh, yes. I believe you." She lifts her coffee cup and takes a sip, before clattering it back onto the saucer with a force that threatens to shatter the china. "I will go along with your ridiculous notion, for now. But please believe *me* when I say I will do everything in my power to avoid marrying you. I *hate* you, Rio, more than I've ever hated anyone in my life. And the thought of being married to you? It turns my stomach. I would rather poke out my eyes with a fork than endure your touch… *Oh…*"

She breaks off as I jump to my feet, and she clutches a hand to her throat when I circle around the table. I grab her by the upper arms and haul her up out of the chair, pulling her against me so there will be no doubt in her mind whatsoever about the effect of her words on me.

She gazes up, her expression a mix of fear, fury, and unwilling desire. The swelling on her injured eye has settled, though the bruising is still forming. In some ways, it makes her unusual eye color stand out more.

When I smile down at her, I can almost hear the growl of rage that I know wants to burst out of her.

"My touch repulses you, does it?" I grind my erection into her stomach, and her eyes half close.

"Your passion can be fueled by pleasure, or it can be fueled by hatred, but you cannot hide your need, Bianca. I sense it, and now you know my response."

"I don't…"

"Oh, little bird. You do." I lean down, testing her, and brush my lips across hers.

A small mewling sound escapes her, and she doesn't pull away.

"I don't *want* to want." Her voice is so faint it is almost not there at all, and her eyes shimmer with unshed tears. "I hate you and everything you stand for."

"I know. And you should. But you will play your part tonight, Bianca, because if you do not…"

"Bastard."

The slap to my cheek comes out of nowhere. I capture her wrist, a surge of arousal hitting me harder than any blow she could ever wield.

This time, when I take her lips, I push the concept of

gentle aside and crush her mouth beneath mine, demanding acquiescence.

There are limits to what I will take, even from her, and Bianca just crossed a line from which there will be no turning back.

For either of us.

"... sex, desire, love, can in some lights seem synonymous,
and in others like elements entirely alien to one another."
Garth Greenwell

Bianca

RIO'S KISS is not about desire. The act is designed to discipline me, pure and simple. All for the fact that I dared raise my hand to him.

I *know* that was the moment I went too far. I would have hit him harder if I hadn't realized that at the very last second and tried to pull back.

Even knowing his motivation stems from punishment, I can't control my goddamn body's response to the delicious, monstrous onslaught.

His presence is so powerful, so strong, that he engulfs me in every way. Even though I hate him—even though part of me wishes he were dead or in jail—I can't hide the fact that there is something about him that switches my body on.

He doesn't need to do anything. He just needs to be nearby, and it's like all my nerve endings light up of their own volition.

I've never felt like that toward anyone, let alone someone I genuinely think is abhorrent.

What is wrong with me? Has the trauma of the past twenty-four hours sent me a little insane?

My mouth automatically opens to let him in, my lips and teeth and tongue beginning a sensual dance with the devil who has dared to invade me in this way. He tastes like coffee, and wine, and some kind of raw male essence that I know is uniquely his.

I hate it, and I love it, in equal measure. I whimper, needing release from the connection, but as if of their own accord, my hands claw at his silk shirt, dragging him in for more.

His scent rises up, a pleasant and spicy juxtaposition to the kiss, like a metaphorical return slap in the face. It's like he is saying, "*This* is what you could have, this strong, sexy, and powerful man who desires you intensely, but *this* is what you deserve—the punishment; the lack of respect. And the proof that I can drag out a response from you, Bianca, whether you want to give me one or not."

Fuck, I hate him.

Fuck. I can't get enough of the bastard.

Somehow, I end up on my ass on the dining room table, crockery and cutlery swept aside in a haphazard mess to make room. My legs splay wide as his erection slides up and down against my core. He is huge, and I wonder what it would feel like if he thrust up and into me with all those firm inches of flesh.

The rush of desire that fans out from our erotic connection is so strong I shudder beneath him.

And still, that punishing kiss goes on.

His fingers dig into my hips, his grip firm as he holds me in place on the polished surface of the table. I clutch at his upper arms, the muscles that ripple beneath my palms only adding to his terrible allure.

When his lips leave mine, I cry out. A wail that contains both self-loathing and need.

You're sick, my mind screams. *You must be, to let him do this to you.*

He nuzzles at my neck, kissing and biting, and damned if I don't tilt back my head to allow him to do so more freely.

A shocked gasp and the smashing of glass are what finally interrupt us.

Rio slowly lifts his head, releasing my neck almost lazily, and turns to the side to stare at whoever has entered.

I don't care who it is. I can't face them, not compromised like this. I half lie there, panting with unfulfilled need, my cheeks so hot I imagine they must be flushed dark, and keep my gaze pinned to the small vee at the base of Rio's throat.

On the surface, he seems unmoved as usual, but this close I note the faster-than-normal tick of his carotid pulse moving the skin of his neck, and I know he is more affected than he's letting on.

He steps back, allowing me room to close my legs and climb down off the table. I bend my head and fuss at my clothing, straightening it for as long as I can, before finally lifting my gaze.

Francine, her eyes still wide, stands in a puddle of something wet, broken glass around her feet. "I was just..." She clears her throat. "They forgot to refill the whiskey, Gregorio. I know you'll want it later..."

Rio waves a dismissive hand. "Get this cleaned up. We will meet our guests in my office, Aunt." His gaze drops briefly to the floor. "With a fresh decanter of whiskey. And cigars. You know Carlos Rossi is partial to a good cigar."

Carlos Rossi? Even I've heard of him. He has been in the news on and off for many years, arrested multiple times on a range of offenses, but somehow never convicted.

A shiver runs down my spine. *That's* the business meeting I'm expected to attend? As Rio's fiancée? I don't want to be here at all, but I particularly do not want to end up on the radar of someone like Carlos Rossi.

But you already are, a little inner voice reminds me. *Rio Agosti is just like him.*

RIO LEADS the way to his office and, not knowing what else to do, I follow like a meek little lamb.

Everywhere in this house, the space is enormous, and his study is no exception. Not only is there a huge desk and executive chair, from where I assume Rio runs his cartel business when he's here, but the walls are lined with shelves full of books intermingled with expensive-looking art pieces, and over to one side is a set of Chesterfield sofas in front of an oversized gas log fireplace.

The marble surround of the fireplace is shiny black, contrasting with the blue-gold flames visible in the hearth. Above the mantel is a painting—a portrait of a couple who bear such a striking resemblance to Rio that I figure they must be his parents.

His dead parents.

His mother had the same dark hair and chiseled bone structure as Rio, though her eyes dance with mischief and her wide mouth lifts in a smile. Is that what Rio would look like if he allowed some emotion in?

His father... I shiver at the flat, cold look in that man's gaze, evident even in the slightly stylized nature of the painting. The artist has captured what I instinctively know must have been very close to real life.

What would it have been like growing up as the eldest son of a man such as that one? Did his mother have much influence or sway in Rio's life, or was he groomed from the beginning to be emotionless and calculating, for that moment when the inevitable happened and the older Agosti lost his grip on power?

I take a seat in the corner of the nearest sofa, while Rio stands with his back to the fireplace, studying me. The leather is cold against my bare skin when I lay my arm along the rolled side, but it soon warms up.

When Francine arrives with liquor and cigars, she asks Rio if he needs me to change into something more formal.

I try not to roll my eyes. I feel so sorry for all the women in this strange Mafia world—it seems as if there is an automatic assumption that none of them can think for themselves. Must the man make all the decisions, even down to what the woman can or can't wear?

I'm tempted to pipe up and say something along those lines until Rio shakes his head. "She is perfect as is. Even with that black eye. Her innocence shines through, which will rile him up more."

I close my mouth on the words I was about to say. I can't decide which shocks me more. His comment about my innocence, or the fact that he said I'm perfect. Neither term is accurate.

After his aunt leaves us alone, I clear my throat. I don't want to admit anything, but I need him to know the facts before his business associates arrive. "I'm not a virgin, Rio, if that's what this is about?"

He grates out a laugh, but there is no humor evident in the sound. "Pity. I would have liked to be your first. But no matter. Your sexual experience is not relevant."

I suppress a shudder at the thought of someone like Rio Agosti taking my virginity. I can't imagine he would ever be gentle enough for that without leaving huge emotional scars, and I'm suddenly grateful for the fumbling encounter with a fellow student in my first year of college. It may not have set my world on fire, but at least the guy was gentle.

"Can you explain to me what this is about, then, please, and what you expect me to say or do?"

"Yes." He sits forward. "Your disappearance all those years ago sparked a series of events, Bianca, that started with a race to secure your family business, and was followed by my parents' untimely murder. Now that I have confirmed your identity, the final piece is about to play out, and our family will have its vengeance."

My gaze automatically lifts to the portrait, and then back to Rio. He studies me without any hint of emotion on his face, despite the gut-wrenching topic. Is he truly incapable of feeling?

"How?"

"Carlos Rossi and my father made a bet. Whoever found the missing Carlotti princess first would bring her into their family and raise her as their own, formally taking the Carlotti business in the process and winning the race to control Boston and beyond."

A race to control Boston? "So, this is about a bet between two crime lords...for control of a *city*?"

"Not just the city. The whole state, Bianca. And even farther afield than that. The stakes are much higher today than they ever were in my father's time."

The nausea that had inexplicably settled somewhat over the course of today suddenly rears up once again in my gut. What will he do if I throw up all over the Chesterfield? Or this fancy rug beneath my feet?

I suck in a breath, trying for control, and attempt an explanation. "I was adopted as a baby. My parents were ordinary folk before my mom passed away in a car crash a couple of years ago. She was a teacher at a local elementary school, and my dad worked in animal rescue for many years. His love for animals led me to my work at Lots of Paws.

"After Mom died, my dad took off to spend time over in Thailand at an animal sanctuary. Doing what he loves is helping him heal from the grief. But I don't hear from him that often anymore as he lives in quite a remote area of the country. Communication is pretty sketchy."

In fact, Dad called me on the morning of my birthday, which means he probably won't even know I'm missing from my usual life for at least another four or five months.

"Your point?"

I clench my teeth before working my jaw to try and release tension. "My point is that I'm not familiar with your world. Even if what you say is true, and I am that...that *person*. I'm sorry your parents died, but I don't know anything about their deaths. I have nothing to do with any of this, and I don't want to be drawn in. Please, Rio. Can you not just let me go now?"

My voice breaks, and the hint of *something* appears behind his eyes. A muscle ticks in his cheek, but then the movement stops and the sense of emptiness in his expression returns. "No. You are heir to the Carlotti cartel, Bianca. You cannot change that fact, even if you want to. I need your inheritance to give me the edge, and to ensure I am in a position to exact revenge for the attack on my family, without risk of reprisals. You must go along with this, for the sake of your friends, your workplace. For *your* sake, in fact. I—"

A discreet knock at the door stops him mid-sentence, and his chest rises and falls in a couple of rapid breaths, as if he has just divulged more than he expected to in this moment.

Despair floods my system. I will not be able to convince him to change his mind.

"Come," he barks out, and a dark-suited man enters the room.

I've seen him before, when I was tied up on the floor of Rio's suite, and then later, hovering in the club. It was *this* man's team who shot my friends and gave me the black eye.

I stand quickly and move around the sofa, putting its solid frame between me and this goon.

"Danelli," Rio says, noting my movement but not commenting on it. "They have arrived?"

"Yes, Boss," the man says, glancing at me with open curiosity before turning back to Rio. "Shall I bring them in?"

"Indeed," Rio answers. "After you've sent in our men. Three teams in here should do it. Let's get this party started, shall we?"

9

"A wise man gets more use from his enemies than a fool from his friends."
Baltasar Gracian

Rio

IT GALLS me to allow Rossi and his men to set foot within my family estate, but my security is at its best in this complex and it makes sense to hold the meeting here.

Besides, now that the word is out about Bianca's identity and whereabouts, I will need everything in my arsenal to keep her safe until our wedding, and the best place to do that is right here.

Rossi enters my office flanked by two of his men, one of whom is Anders. The others are waiting at the front gates in a bunch of SUVs, not allowed to cross the threshold of my property.

He was told two could accompany him, and that is what I have allowed.

Rossi is short and rotund, balding these days, and deceptively friendly in his countenance. Underneath the grandfatherly façade, he is as ruthless as me.

And that makes him a dangerous enemy.

He makes a beeline for me then stops short when he notices Bianca. She seems to have shrunk into herself, pressing back into one of the walls and wrapping her arms around her middle.

Rossi's brows rise almost comically high. I allow myself a slow smile. I know what he's seeing, and I know why shock contorts his features for a second before the bland mask descends once again.

I have a photograph in my possession of Bianca's mother, Rina, and if not for the unstyled nature of Bianca's long hair compared to the sleek bob that her mother wore, she and Rina could be twins.

Rossi knew Rina well, by all accounts, and I know I won't need to show him the DNA results to convince him that Bianca Carlotti stands in the room with us right now.

"Carlos."

"Rio. Good to see you, old friend." Rossi approaches more slowly than before, darting glances between me and Bianca.

When he reaches me, he holds out a hand for a shake. I stare at him, unmoving, until he drops the hand and wipes it awkwardly on the side of his trousers.

"Yes. Well. You have had my apology already, but now you have it in person. A misunderstanding, Rio, and it won't happen again."

"An attempted shooting is not a misunderstanding,

Carlos."

"No. No indeed."

I step forward and gesture at the sofa, waiting until he is seated before I sit opposite. His men stand nearby, watchful and impassive, just as my three teams do the same from different vantage points around the room.

At a nod from me, Danelli brings over a tray containing whiskey, glasses, and the Cuban cigar humidor I keep for occasions such as this.

Once drinks are poured and we have cut and lit our cigars, I allow a moment for enjoyment and watch the trail of smoke waft upward from the cigar end.

Then I turn to Bianca and hold out my free hand. I hope she can read the message in my eyes.

Behave, little bird.

"Come, my darling. I wish to introduce you."

Her teeth work at her bottom lip for a moment, but after a brief hesitation in which her eyes narrow and I can sense her urge to disobey me, she shifts off the wall and walks over to me with slightly jerky movements. She takes a seat beside me, so close I can feel the trembling of her leg against mine. I clasp her fingers and lay our joined hands atop her thigh.

"Carlos Rossi, meet Bianca Carlotti. My fiancée."

"Charmed, my dear, I am sure." Rossi dips his head and then offers a wolfish grin that shows almost all his teeth.

Bianca recoils, then seems to rally, sitting up straighter. Her trembling fades to nothing.

Unexpected pride rises in my chest. Whatever she is or isn't, this girl has a great deal of inner fortitude.

It is such a pity she is merely a pawn in this game. But that is the way of our world.

"Likewise." Bianca's voice is abrupt, as if she has to force the word out past some kind of barrier in her throat.

She looks down at our clasped hands, and I hold on more tightly when I feel her begin to pull out of my grasp.

"Did Rio tell you I knew your mother when she was young, my dear? Such a lovely woman. You are the spitting image of Rina."

"Rina." She repeats the name, this time in a more natural tone, and then looks up at Rossi. "You knew her? That's very interesting. Did you know my father, too? What was his name?"

"You haven't told her much, Rio, have you? Shame. Your father's name was Stefano, my dear."

Bianca nods slowly. "Stefano. And Rina. Did you kill them, Mr. Rossi? Did you kill my birth mother and father?"

Bianca

RIO'S HAND jerks on my leg, the only indication of his shock at what I've just asked.

But I have to know. Now that the can of worms has been opened, I need to know more about my birth parents. And what happened to them.

If either of the two men seated on this couch with me had anything to do with their deaths, I will do everything in my power to bring them down.

I will destroy them for destroying my family.

The words reverberate around my brain as if they have come from someplace else altogether. What am I thinking? This is not me, thinking of revenge and plotting the destruction of other people. This is the sort of thing Rio might say.

I've only been in this world a day and a bit, and it is already warping my thinking.

"Well?" I push, knowing I shouldn't, but unable to stop. "Did you kill them, Mr. Rossi?"

"I will forgive you this time, my dear. Because you are Rina's daughter. And because..." His gaze flicks to Rio and back. "Because you are *his* fiancée. But do not push me on this. I did not kill your parents. I loved Stefano like a brother, and I loved your mother..." His left eye twitches, just slightly, before he adds quietly, "Yes. I loved your mother dearly."

I study the old man sitting across from Rio and me, and for some reason, I believe him. There was a note in his voice just then that alerted me...

"You didn't love my mother like a *sister*, then?"

He sucks in a sharp breath and releases it slowly. "No," he admits. "I did not love her in that way, like a sister. I was devastated when..."

He breaks off, and to my shock, he pulls out a handkerchief and dabs at his eyes. What the hell? Did I just make a mob boss cry?

Rio pats my thigh as if pleased with me and releases my hand, shifting back to sit more comfortably on the sofa.

Tension that I hadn't even realized was permeating the air in the room relaxes a notch. Even the security goons scattered everywhere look slightly less edgy when I glance around.

That is, until Rio opens his mouth and speaks. "We would be delighted if you would attend our wedding, Carlos, to watch us unite in holy matrimony. Will you be our guest? My *friend*."

There is steel in his tone, and hell could freeze over with

the amount of ice that suddenly descends back into the air around us all.

"Of course, Rio. I would be delighted," Carlos says. His expression suggests otherwise. He is clearly unhappy at Rio's invitation. "You are a very lucky man. When is the special day?"

"Next Thursday," Rio says smoothly, and my mouth drops open.

Today is Saturday, by my reckoning, given my birthday was on Friday. Was it only yesterday that I was snatched off the street?

My birthday, I remember, with a hollow feeling in the pit of my stomach, was the day I was supposed to celebrate a bright and rosy future, and possibly an upcoming date with Dave. Instead, I am sitting here in a Mafia boss's compound, discussing my marriage next week with men who kill others at the drop of a hat.

Men who shot my friends.

Monsters who destroy lives while chatting over liquor and stupid cigars that stink out the room.

Then a thought strikes my brain, and I turn to look at Rio. No way could he possibly have a marriage license sorted in that short time frame.

He smiles smugly as if guessing my thoughts.

Of course. He probably has a whole set of city officials in his pocket. He only has to click his fingers, or get one of his minions to call, and the paperwork will all be in place in an instant.

I stand and move to the fireplace, staring into the grate and praying for calm. I feel as if I'm about to have a panic attack, and I do not want to lose control at that level in front of these people.

I focus on the dancing flames, studying their tiny blue gas-lit centers surrounded by golden orange light, and breathe. In. Out. In and out. Keep going. Don't panic. Not in front of Rio or Carlos Rossi.

After what feels like forever, but is probably only a handful of seconds, my heart rate calms, and my breathing slows to a more normal rhythm. But I don't know how much longer I can hold on to my emotions without breaking apart into what feels like a million little pieces.

There has been far too much to deal with since yesterday. And I suspect tomorrow will bring more of the same. Or worse.

As if Rio is somehow tuned in to my inner turmoil, he suddenly appears by my side. "You should rest, darling. It is late. Carlos and I have further business to discuss, but it does not need to concern you. Head to bed. I shall see you later."

His tone and his words hint to all in the room that we are already intimate as a couple, and anger builds, burning out the panic.

He places a hand on my back, splaying out his fingers and caressing me gently, and then bends to kiss my cheek. "You did well, little bird. I was proud of you tonight."

Those words are only for me, whispered into my ear in a way that warms my skin.

It is lucky for him that I am facing away from his guest because I can't stop a grimace of pure disgust.

I feel rather than hear his almost silent chuckle as he moves his lips to my temple, and his breath warms me there, too.

He knows, as well as I do, that my grimace was not because I hate his touch.

But because I don't.

73

"... she felt the energy between them shift, like a serpent circling back on itself, swallowing itself whole, anger and passion feeding off one another."
Sylvain Reynard

Bianca

RIO LEAVES me alone for the next few days, but in some ways that is worse, not better, because I remain on tenterhooks, not knowing when or where he will surface and decide to strike.

My hope that someone will have reported me missing and the police will already be searching for me after the abduction is short-lived.

Francine delivered me breakfast in my room the morning after I met Rossi and threw a parting shot over her shoulder as she left.

"Do not think that anyone has missed you, Bianca. Our

family has a long reach, and loose ends are already tied. You could stay here in this compound for the next two years, and no one would question your whereabouts."

Then she left, leaving me alone to ponder what the hell she meant by *loose ends are tied*.

Friends, neighbors, and work colleagues silenced... *How*? With money? Threats? More bullets?

I keep reliving that moment I was shoved in the trunk of the car, and hearing the *pop, pop, pop* of a gun. Imagining Dave and Shelley lying on the pavement, bleeding out in front of the workplace we all love so much. My limbs tremble every time the terrible images flicker to life in my head.

And in the silence of my suite, my hatred of Rio grows.

I decide to demand answers of him when he returns, but of course, he does no such thing.

It's like he knows I'm brewing for a fight and wants to avoid the possibility of that at all costs before our wedding day arrives.

The day of our wedding. *Tomorrow*.

My stomach clenches at the realization that this time tomorrow, Gregorio Agosti will be my husband. And if I refuse to go along with the marriage charade, others will suffer the consequences.

Will ours be a marriage in name only? A business transaction? Or will he expect more? Will he expect me to share his bed, give him my body as well as my inheritance?

My insides wobble at the thought, but I don't have time to dwell on what that means. A whole army of women have surrounded me since midmorning, measuring my body and my feet, holding up swatches of fabric that have already been crafted into magnificent bridal dresses, trying on shoes, and color-matching cosmetics against my skin, lips, and eyes.

At one point I am shoved down into a chair and, while the fabric and dress people fuss on the other side of the room, a hairdresser steps up and begins to snip at the ends of my hair in what she mutters is "a well-overdue tidy-up." In front of me, a nail technician using a portable table soaks my nails in readiness for some kind of manicure process.

The technician calls it dipping powder and tuts over the state of my hands. "You look like you've had years of hard manual labor, hon," she says, shaking her head. "What have you been doing?"

I can't be bothered trying to explain that long and expensively manicured nails do not usually work well in a rescue shelter for animals. "I've never had a manicure."

"Obviously. Well, we'll need to do tips, too," she says. "French style?"

"Do whatever you want."

I try not to take out my frustration on these service providers. It's not their fault the man who hired them for this sham event is a monster. But I can't help probing just a little. Testing out every possibility for escape, no matter how futile it may seem.

"While you finish that hand, would you mind if I borrow your phone just to make a quick call?" I ask. "I seem to have misplaced mine."

At my question, all sound and activity in the room ceases as if a switch has been flicked.

The technician's eyes narrow as she stares at me, then she dips her head over my hand. "Not happening."

Oh. So, these people *are* on Rio's payroll, not just casual hires. Is there anyone in the whole of Boston who isn't?

The hairdresser bends and murmurs in my ear, "Be very

careful, dear. This world is not one you can escape from once you're in it."

An icy shiver traverses my body, and I don't seem able to move of my own volition after that. Except when each of them asks me to do something, and I will myself to pretend I'm not frozen with fear.

Drop my head forward, lift my fingers, close one eye while they try out a different set of fake lashes. Stand up and strip off to my underwear so they can check that the small alterations they've completed on the chosen dress actually make the garment fit properly.

Someone hands me a plate of food at one point and tells me to eat. I do, but afterward, I have no idea what was on the plate.

Eventually, they all seem satisfied and file out of my suite, promising to return early tomorrow in time for the real event.

I'm left alone, standing in the middle of the floor, with my perfectly manicured, French-tipped nails, my new and supposedly much improved hairdo, and rage beginning to boil deep down inside me—rage that burns away the frozen feeling and stops the terror from rising.

I feed the rage with everything I have inside me. My hands clench, the new nails digging into my palms.

A pair of strappy sandals sits on the couch, left behind by one of the dressers.

I pick up one of the ivory-colored heels, hefting it in my hand. "*Fuck them all!*"

Then I turn and throw it straight at the large mirror above the fireplace. The shoe hits and splinters the mirror into fragments which rain down all over the floor.

Seven years of bad luck for breaking a mirror? Couldn't get any worse than my current situation, surely?

"Temper, temper, Bianca." The smooth, deep voice comes from behind me, and I whirl to find Rio standing just inside the door.

His arms are folded across his chest as he leans against the wall in a casual pose. A derisive smirk decorates his face.

Without thinking, I grab up the second shoe and hurl it at him, screaming in his direction. "*Bastard*! I fucking *hate* you! Let me leave, you fucking—"

"Enough!" He pushes off the wall in an instant, ducking as the shoe sails over his shoulder.

And then he comes at me. Fast.

I try to turn and run, but he grabs my arms before I can swivel. My momentum, and his, carries us, and I stumble back and fall onto the couch with Rio landing on top of me.

His weight crushes the air out of my chest, and our limbs tangle up together.

I can't draw in breath at all, but I don't care. I've had enough. I kick and struggle underneath him, huffing to get air and growling anything I manage to inhale straight back out again. I have no idea what has taken over me, except to know deep down that this must be how it feels to reach the end of your tolerance.

His expression, livid to start with, slowly morphs into amusement, and then something else altogether.

Desire.

I read it deep behind his normally deadpan eyes as he stares down at me, and I still, suddenly aware of the huge erection pressing against my belly.

Oh, hell. Did my wriggling and cursing cause that?

He shifts his weight slightly, and it becomes easier to breathe, but he doesn't climb off me.

Instead, he settles more comfortably, until the hardness of his arousal presses into my mound, placing pressure directly on my clit and effectively pinning me beneath him.

I am unable to move, because if I do, I will rub on him, inciting the sensations between my legs to escalate, and I don't want that at all.

"Your passion is fiery, more so than I expected," he says, the puff of his breath caressing my lips. "It's a turn-on."

"It's not passion." I study his firm chin, his angular cheeks, and note the way his mouth has a cruel yet sensual cast. I look anywhere but at his eyes. Those dark, desire-filled eyes. "It's anger."

His lip curves up at one corner, and I can't help myself. I raise my gaze to his.

This close, I realize for the first time that the eyes I thought were almost black are, in fact, an attractive chocolate brown. He has fine lines at the corners, like most people beyond a certain age, I guess, but I hadn't expected any vulnerability whatsoever, and the lines suggest a hint of human susceptibility.

I become breathless for a whole other reason altogether. Lying like this, for just a few seconds, he seems to offer something more than the heartless mob boss persona.

I bite at my bottom lip, moistening the area with the tip of my tongue, and shift slightly, forgetting not to. The rush of desire between my legs is so strong I almost moan out loud.

Then his pupils flare, and the sense of vulnerability and something human is gone. The darkness returns to his expression.

"Are they not interlinked, little bird? Passion and anger. Just like pleasure and pain."

"Not in my world," I manage, and he smiles gently, as if I've just said something ridiculous.

"The thing is, Bianca, you are not *in* your world anymore. From now on, you're a part of mine."

Rio

WHEN SHE PARTS her lips like that, darting out with the very tip of her pink tongue to moisten them, it takes everything in me not to crush her mouth beneath mine.

Until she moves her hips, inadvertently grinding against my erect cock, and my control dips.

"Bianca." Her name comes out half strangled, and I lower my head and sweep my tongue across her mouth, wanting to taste what she is unconsciously offering.

She closes her eyes, as if she cannot bear to look at me this close, but does nothing to avoid my brief invasion.

"Why are you here tonight?" Her voice is the merest whisper. "Isn't it bad luck, the night before the wedding, for the groom to see…"

She swallows, clearly unable to finish.

"Bad luck? You just smashed a mirror, little bird."

"Ah yes. So I did."

I shift my weight more onto my right arm so I can lift a finger of my left hand to trace a line down her throat. So delicate. I rest my hand there, my fingers spread, and both of us know I could squeeze tightly if I wanted to, and there'd be nothing she could do to stop me.

She swallows again in a convulsive manner that vibrates beneath my grip, and I wonder if she has ever had a man thrust deeply into that space. Thrust deeply and claim her throat with his cock?

As if she can sense the direction of my thoughts, her eyes flash open, and my heart skips in a strange pattern at the close-up reminder of her unusual coloring. The darker ring of iris around the delicious golden center. Brown eyes, but nothing like any other brown eyes I've ever seen.

"A bad portent for our marriage, Rio, isn't it? All this bad luck? Perhaps you should just let me go." Her lips lift in a tiny smile, but her brows dip into a frown. "I will sign over the papers for whatever you want. You can have my inheritance. My Mafia family fortune, or the official rights to the Carlotti name, or whatever it is you need from me. I'll give it to you freely, if you simply let me go."

"No."

"But—"

I stop her futile protest with a kiss. A short but intense kiss in which I claim her mouth the way I do with all the other women I've ever had. Hard and forceful, and with no regard for anything but stamping her with possession.

Mine.

She whimpers, the sound as effective as a face slap when it reverberates up from her throat and into mine. I involuntarily soften my approach, trying to gauge why that sound affects me so strongly.

Then she whimpers again, but there's a different note in the sound this time—a note that sends a signal straight to my groin. All of a sudden, her hands clutch at my back, her nails digging into me through my shirt, and she pulls me close.

Then she kisses me back.

The embrace changes completely to something I don't know what to do with. It is no longer led by me in a ruthless show of possession. Instead, her lips and tongue against mine are sensual, delicate, coaxing an altogether different response from me.

What is she doing? Now I'm the one groaning as she takes my sounds into her mouth, her throat, and her legs shift beneath me, opening wider until her thighs cradle my hips.

Her fragrance rises up around me, instilling the moment with something almost innocent. Something with which I am completely unfamiliar.

I need to extricate myself from this. But I can't. She's too potent.

I keep kissing her, being kissed by her, wanting more. Wanting to reach into her innocence and let it wash over me until the sins of my life are erased.

There is no pain in this embrace, only pleasure. This is not passion. Or anger.

I don't know what this is.

But I have to shut it down now, before she brings me undone.

11

"*Marriage is the dark side of the honeymoon.*"
Marilyn Monroe

Bianca

I CAN'T FIGURE out if I'm going to throw up, faint, or have a heart attack and die of stress right here in the entrance of the wedding chapel.

The picturesque building is situated on the grounds of Rio's estate, surrounded by natural beauty. And yet, inside, within these four stone walls that press in so hard I can barely breathe, the ugly lie is about to play out.

I'm going to marry a Mafia crime boss against my will— a man who may have killed my parents. Normal wedding day jitters ain't got nothing on this scenario.

As I stare down the aisle toward the altar, loneliness hits me anew. I don't know anyone in the pews, except Francine, seated in the front row next to a young man who looks like her. Presumably her son Tommaso. Rio's cousin.

And there, of course, is Carlos Rossi, seated about halfway down the aisle on the side of the chapel normally allocated to the bride.

Interesting.

A sea of strange faces stare at me with undisguised curiosity as Rio's right-hand man Danelli—his second, they call him—grips my upper arm tightly and practically hauls me down the aisle slightly faster than the stately wedding music dictates.

The dress chosen for me is a strapless, floor-length design in ivory satin, hugging my figure so tightly that I worry the seams may split if I have to sit down later in the day. A long tulle veil billows out behind me, attached to a diamond circlet that sits atop my hair which has been left to fall down my back in perfectly styled waves.

I thought the circlet was fake when they brought it out. Diamantes rather than real stones. Until the team assigned to dress me all began to laugh when I made the mistake of mentioning that. I can only imagine how much the little crown is worth—probably more than my year's wages, I'm betting.

Everything about this situation is equal parts farcical and horrifying. Is there anyone here who will speak up for me? Tell these crazy people that it isn't okay to snatch someone off the street and then arrange to marry them only a scant week later?

I run my gaze over every face, looking for a hint of sympathy or support. There is none. Instead, beneath the curiosity, I see indifference, calculation, annoyance. Underlying it all, there is a hint of fear that permeates the air.

Are they all so afraid of Rio? Is he truly that vicious that he can hold a whole chapel full of people at ransom as he does whatever he likes?

Perhaps the fear is all mine.

I take deep breaths as I get closer to the altar and let the air out slowly each time. Reminding myself not to panic. Reminding myself that I may be stuck in this nightmare situation for now, but I'm not dead yet.

While I can still breathe, I will never accept this state of affairs as my new reality. Rio may force me to marry him today and take ownership of my heritage, but he will never own *me*.

That is the vow I make to myself as I raise my chin and meet his eyes. *You may soon possess my body, but you will never own my soul.*

He is in a formal black suit with a black shirt instead of the standard wedding white. His attire, together with the wink of diamonds at his cuffs, all speak to luxury, wealth, and power. He oozes sex appeal, and the punch of desire to my belly is unexpected.

I stumble on my last couple of steps. Danelli grips my arm, steadies me, and then releases me to Rio before shifting away. Rio stares down at me with approval, and with the hard edge of emotion glittering in the depths of his expression.

I am so deep in Rio's eyes that movement at his side startles me. Rio's younger brother Nikolas. I haven't yet officially met him, but Francine mentioned in one of her brief visits to my rooms that Nikolas would support Rio today, standing at his side.

I flick a glance at the brother before focusing back on Rio. Nikolas is not quite a mirror image of his older brother, with longer tousled hair and a more casual air, but in a dark suit and tie, he is still starkly handsome, though without the underlying sense of menacing power that emanates from Rio.

Nicky, Francine called him, her gaze softening when she mentioned him. He returned home from a business trip for this event, apparently. He is clearly not as powerful or revered as Rio within the family, but presumably, he must have some redeeming features to inspire such a look of affection from his aunt.

There's another brother, I remember, named Luca, but apparently, he couldn't make it home in time. Nor could Rio's sister, according to Francine. I will meet them soon, I've been told, but not today for our wedding.

Does it even matter? This isn't a real wedding.

I stare hard at Rio, trying to contain the rage and pour all of my fear and loathing for him into my expression.

As soon as I get away from you, I will organize an annulment.

And a police-raiding party.

He studies me intently, his mouth wide and flat and his eyes dark above those honed cheekbones that give him a haughty air. Another wave of desire kicks me right in the gut. I've only ever seen him in suits and dressy clothing, so today should be no different than any other day.

And yet, it is.

I have never been more attracted to a man in my life, and I have never been more desperate to run away from him, as far and as fast as I can.

Too late. His hand takes mine, and I am in his grip—about to become another of his possessions—and there is nothing I can do to stop this charade, unless I want to ruin the lives of people and businesses I care about.

"You are truly beautiful, Bianca." His words are quiet,

surprisingly directed at me rather than the watching crowd, and I am instantly transported back to last night, to the moment his kiss changed from punishing to seductive.

The moment I gave in and began to kiss him back.

The moment his hand wandered down and slipped inside my sweatpants, an exploring finger finding and circling my already engorged clit.

I remember how I arched up into his palm, moaning into his mouth and hearing an answering groan in return. How I tore my mouth from his, gasping as he flicked my bud back and forth, then slid his finger down my already wet seam, gathering moisture, before sliding deep into my channel as if he belonged there.

As if he already owned that space.

The invasion felt wrong, and yet, so right. I hovered there, right on the precipice of orgasm, for what felt like forever, but then he thrust in and out with his finger slightly curved, and as simply as that, I fell over the edge into an explosion of pleasure that tore through my body.

When my climax faded and my shudders ceased, he leaned down and kissed my cheek.

"You are beautiful, Bianca. Especially when you come. And to think, that was only one finger."

Just like that, the spell broke. I turned my head to the side and wiped my mouth on my T-shirt-covered shoulder before facing him again.

"I hate you more than I've ever hated anyone. I hate that my body responds to you when my brain doesn't want it. Hate it with a passion."

"Ah, there it is. You see? Passion and anger. It was hovering there for us both, after all."

Laughter shook his whole frame, and as he rolled off me and stood, I wished I had the strength to fight him properly.

He reached into a pocket and pulled out his phone, pushing a couple of buttons before shoving the screen into my line of sight. "Just a little reminder, beautiful Bianca, of why your cooperation is so vital tomorrow."

I tried to look anywhere else but at the image on his phone screen, but of course, I couldn't avoid it. The Lots of Paws front entrance loomed in my vision.

"I wish you were dead, Rio Agosti." I spat the words at him as he tucked away his phone and strolled to the door.

My only comfort in that moment was that, unlike me, he had not experienced climax. I hoped he would trip over on the way out and break that massive erect piece of flesh right off his body.

"No doubt you will get your wish one day, Bianca."

"And I hope that one day," I yelled, as he opened the door and stepped out into the hallway, "I might be the one to kill you."

I focus on that thought as we exchange our wedding vows in the chapel.

Rio

IT IS DONE. Bianca Carlotti is my wife, the act witnessed by everyone who needed to see me preserve the power base of the Agosti family and formally unite our clans. Formally, and within the law.

Her eyes spat vitriol as she agreed to the vows, and at one stage Nicky leaned over to murmur into my ear, "I would not fall asleep beside that one, brother. You might not wake up."

I speared him with a look intended to shut him up, but he simply shrugged and grinned at me. "Your funeral, Rio."

Nicky is the only person I allow any leeway when it comes to teasing. I trust him with my life.

The reception in my estate's ballroom is in full swing, and I sense the growing trepidation in Bianca, seated beside me at the head table. Her leg jerks up and down as her foot taps constantly on the floor. The movement beneath the table linen is hidden from all except me.

She looks up at me at one point, her eyes mostly curtained by long lashes. "Are you..." She stops, swallows. "Will you...tonight..."

Understanding dawns. She isn't yet sure if I intend to claim my marital rights, and the uncertainty is driving her tension upward.

"I have not yet decided."

"Oh. Okay." Her gaze drops to her plate, on which the food remains mostly untouched.

She does things to me, makes me feel more than I want to. And in my position, it is dangerous to succumb to emotion. Feelings and sentiment make you weak, an easier target for any enemies looking for a crack in the armor.

Glancing at the guests, I calculate quickly. Probably eighty percent would not be unhappy to see me dead. The other twenty percent could not care either way.

I cannot afford to get close to Bianca. Not in that way, with sentiment. It will weaken me.

Physical closeness, on the other hand, is safer. That kiss last night... The way her mouth opened near the end, the way her face screwed up as if in agony, the half-strangled, gasping groan that erupted at the moment she orgasmed around my finger...

Fuck. My cock remembers all too well. My swelling flesh strains against my trousers, full and throbbing.

I place a hand atop the one of Bianca's nearest to me on the tabletop and squeeze, hard. "We need to dance soon, wife. It is expected."

"Dance?" She turns those beautiful eyes up to mine once again, and the trepidation in them is obvious.

"Indeed. The wedding dance." I cannot wait to get her into my arms, and yet control will be paramount.

I need to show the guests, most of whom are business colleagues or rivals, that my armor has no weak spot. My mouth tightens at the thought of what may happen if someone perceives a crack.

"There will be people coming up to us with streamers. If they hand anything to you, take it. They may wind the streamers around us, as well. Just go along with that if it happens. It is tradition."

"Oh. Streamers. Sure." She frowns. "I haven't heard of that tradition before."

"Have you attended many Italian weddings?"

"Well. No. I haven't attended any weddings. Until today."

The sudden sadness in her tone incites annoyance. I don't question whether the emotion is directed at her or myself. Instead, I shut it down and stand, dragging her to her feet.

I nod at the quartet in the corner who've been diligently playing dinner music. A silence falls, and then a wedding waltz starts up, and everyone turns in their seats and begins to clap and cheer, watching as I take my wife onto the floor.

"You are marrying into great wealth, Bianca," I murmur, as I lead her into the first steps of our wedding dance.

When I draw her fully into my arms and against my body, her soft curves seem to fit perfectly. That citrus scent of hers wafts up into my nostrils, and I can't help the quick inhale. Drawing more of her in, despite my intention to stay disconnected.

"I will look after you, as my wife," I add, with an uncharacteristic urge to be kind.

She stiffens, then slumps a little, allowing me to whirl her around. "I'm sure you will," she says, her words slightly muffled against my chest. "As one of your possessions. Not as a real person, with feelings and needs and *desires*…"

She breaks off, coughing slightly as if regretting that final word.

I allow myself a savage grin above her head, fighting for control even as my cock swells once again. There is no way she can avoid feeling *that* against her belly.

"Desires? I will look after those, too, Bianca. And I will introduce you to *new* desires…ones your innocent little brain never dreamed of before now."

Her head jerks back, and finally, her earlier feistiness is back, pushing the trepidation away. Her eyes communicate fire, but nothing comes out of her open mouth except a huff of breath.

Then we are no longer alone on the dance floor, crowded by others as people press streamer ends into our hands. Her fist clenches tightly as she grips a streamer, and then I whirl her again, winding us tight in the paper bindings that symbolize the truth.

Bianca Carlotti is mine now. All mine.

And no one will ever break apart the Agosti-Carlotti cartel again.

1 2

"It's not what you look at that matters, it's what you see."
Henry David Thoreau

Bianca

I WILL INTRODUCE you to new desires...ones your innocent brain never dreamed of. His taunting words play in my head, over and over, while I wait for my husband to come to my suite.

Husband? That word alone sends shards of horror down my spine.

I am married to mob boss Gregorio Agosti.

Never in a million years would I ever have dreamed of such a thing coming to pass. Will Rio want to claim his marital rights? Will I let him if he tries?

I pace before the windows in my sitting room, back and forth, watching the twinkling lights out in the vast garden and the bobbing of boats at the formerly empty river jetty. The throb of music rolls up from somewhere down below, where visitors are still partying, celebrating the wedding of Rio Agosti and his cartel-building bride.

Me.

Fuck.

How has this possibly happened? How will I get out of this? *Will* I ever get out of this situation...alive?

My stomach churns, and I clench my fists as I continue to stride the length of the room and back again, wondering how many guards are stationed out there in the darkness. More than the usual number, I bet. Given the stature of the guest list downstairs.

"Wait for me upstairs, little bird," Rio whispered after our wedding dance finished, before lifting one of my hands to his lips and kissing my knuckles.

I hadn't been able to control my shudder that denoted both distaste and desire. The push-pull of both is destroying me from the inside out.

"I will be up to tuck you into bed. When I am ready for you."

His eyes in that moment were no longer deadpan. Instead, they glittered with promise. A promise that is tearing me apart.

I want him here, if only to get it over with. And I don't want him here, because his presence will ignite these strange needs in my body, and I don't want to acknowledge anything positive about being kidnapped and forced into marriage with a man like Rio Agosti.

I hate him. *I hate him.* But there's no denying it now, either to him or to myself. I desire him, too.

And that desire fuels my hatred even more.

I wish he were dead.

The clock high up on the wall in a corner of the suite hits eleven, and I release a sigh. He is staying away on purpose. I'm sure of it. We were married at 2:00 p.m., and it has been hours since the guests waved me out of the reception area.

"Fuck you, asshole." I spit the words out, as vitriolic as if he were standing in front of me. It's easy to be defiant when you're on your own. "I'm not waiting up any longer."

I march to the bathroom and tear off the stupid wedding gown, uncaring of whether or not I rip it in the process. Not like anyone will ever wear the damn thing again. I scrub at my face until it is free of makeup, and then peel off the ridiculous whore-like underwear that they dressed me in earlier today. Finally, I am naked. I breathe a sigh of relief.

At last, I can be me again.

At least for a little while. Until *he* arrives.

I wonder if they have any flannel PJs or even an old T-shirt in the changing area? I am chuckling at the absurdity of my own thoughts as I emerge from the bathroom, and then stop short when I realize I'm no longer alone.

"*Rio!*"

He stands inside the door of the suite, his jacket and tie already gone. His eyes widen, just for a split second, as he rakes my nudity from head to toe. He seems just as shocked as me, then the fleeting glimpse of the real Rio is gone, and he's back to being impassive.

I clutch my arms across my front, but the gesture is obviously futile.

Then he sweeps across the space, closing the distance between us before I can do more than suck in a ragged breath and curl my toes into the carpet in a vain attempt to anchor myself to something. Anything.

Strong arms fold around me, dragging me in against a hard body, and then his mouth claims mine in a way that leaves no doubt in either of our minds.

I am his.

And there is nothing I can do to change that fact.

The worst thing—the *very* worst—is that in this moment, there is nothing I *want* to do to change it.

Rio

HER MOUTH OPENS to my onslaught, letting me in and responding as if she can't get enough of me.

I can't get enough of her.

Her acquiescence shocks me. And yet, it also doesn't. I sense the need in her, and guess that she doesn't know what to do with it. She has probably never tapped into that side of herself. We are going to have some fun, Bianca and me, when she moves beyond her current state of rage toward acceptance of her situation.

Our mouths devour each other as if we're starved of oxygen and the other is our life source. Her lips and tongue dance with mine while her sweet taste fills my senses.

A moan slips up her throat and into my mouth. I swallow the sound and return it as an involuntary groan.

We break apart, my breath shuddering in my chest. I drag in air. She shivers in my arms, panting, but I know she isn't cold. Her skin beneath my hands when I run them up and down her naked body is warm and smooth.

I clutch at her bare ass, kneading her flesh, keeping her as close as humanly possible to the seat of my need even as my trouser material still separates us.

My cock aches in its fabric confines. The need to fill her, to possess her, pushes in on me from all directions. I must have Bianca—my *wife*—before this night is done.

I must have her *now*, before the need drives me insane and destroys any semblance of control I have left.

What is it about her that pulls me in so completely?

When I entered the suite and saw her emerge with that wry chuckle softening her fierce expression, her pale skin and subtle curves framed by the golden light from the bathroom, my breath stuttered to a stop even as my heart rate ratcheted up to dangerous levels.

She does something to me, this woman, and it is time to sate the desire.

I begin to unbutton my shirt, but she pushes my fingers aside, taking over the task even as her angry eyes burn into mine.

I move my hands to my trousers, undoing the fastenings and letting them drop, allowing her to push aside my shirt and remove it, before quickly stepping out of the rest of my clothing.

My cock springs up as soon as it is released, proclaiming how much I want her. Her gaze drops to my erection and holds there, as if fascinated. She licks her lips, her beautiful lips, and then her eyes dart back up to mine.

Oh, yes.

"On your knees, little bird," I command, only there's a hoarse note in my voice that I can't disguise. For the first time in my life, I feel a sense of vulnerability in front of another human being. It confuses me. I don't like it. I push her down to the floor more forcefully than I intend. "In your mouth. Now."

Her hands on my thighs tremble; she looks up through her lashes, a luscious curtain that briefly hides the anger and hatred usually seated in her eyes. Then her lips lift at one corner in that wry expression I am beginning to enjoy.

"Be afraid, Rio. I might bite it off."

She sinks onto me before I can respond, taking me deep into her mouth and throat, and I can only groan as her hot wetness coats me, and the sensation of being licked and sucked destroys any rational thought.

I groan again as her tongue flicks the head of my cock, and my desire ratchets up toward incendiary.

Yes, I am afraid. I admit it, deep down inside.

I am afraid of what you are doing to me, Bianca Carlotti-Agosti.

But I will never say that out loud. Not to her. Not to anyone.

13

"Sometimes the person you want the most, is the person you're best without."
Unknown

Bianca

I WORK ON INSTINCT. I've never given head before. I don't even know why I'm doing this so readily, so easily, as if I've done it a thousand times before. As if I can't get enough of the guy.

As if I love him.

They say love and hate are closely entwined. Maybe that's it? Whatever the reason, I can't seem to help myself. My whole body is on fire with need. I've never felt anything like the urges that rise up and overwhelm me as I taste and suck on Rio's rigid flesh.

This is my husband. My *husband.*

He forced me into marriage, and I don't want to be here.

I *could* bite hard. Destroy his masculinity. At the very least, I could make him bleed so much that I may have the chance to run and hide from the monster I've just married.

He is aware of it, too. I see the knowledge in his eyes as he stares down at me, his fingers tangling in a jerky motion in my hair. I hear it in those insane-sounding groans and growls erupting from his chest and throat.

And therein lies the dilemma. I want to hurt him; I hate him for what he's done. What he *is*. But in this moment, where he has made himself vulnerable and handed over that vulnerability to my keeping, something stays me.

I want this. I've never wanted this so much in my life.

I want his scent around me, on me, in me, as his desire rises to meet mine.

I want to taste his hot, salty flesh, not knowing who has been here before me. Not caring.

I am so wet between my legs I can feel the moisture seeping down to coat my thighs. I reach down a hand to explore, and my fingers slip and slide everywhere before finding and caressing my clit.

I arch my back, the twin sensations of my own hand and his hard flesh in my mouth almost too much to bear. As if he can sense how close I am to losing control, he suddenly stops the movement of my head with a firm hand and slides his cock out of my mouth. Then he lifts me up, right up, as if I'm made of mere feathers. Until I'm high enough to wrap my legs around his waist and my breasts mush against his firm chest.

"From now on, you do not touch yourself unless I say so," he growls against my lips. "Your pussy is *mine*."

He takes my mouth again, kissing me hard, and I release a

gasp into him as his fingers reach around and dip into my seam from the rear. He slides up and down in my wetness. It feels different when *he* touches me there. So different.

I grind against his six-pack.

Then I jerk as he shifts his hand and smacks my ass cheek. Not gentle. Enough to leave a sting burning my flesh. He does it again, then he is back to my seam, dipping again into the wetness that I can't seem to control.

Fuck. I want this. I want *him*. So. Much.

But why? How is my body betraying me like this? So fully and completely?

"I hate you." I breathe the words against his neck, and hot tears fill my eyes.

I will not goddamn fucking cry. Not now. Not over *this*.

"I know. And it fuels my desire, Bianca. You have no. Fucking. Idea."

He pushes into my channel with one finger, and I stiffen in his arms, my body shuddering almost involuntarily at the invasion. His lips trail down my neck, and my head tips back, allowing him easier access. A second finger pushes inside me, and I release a moan. He walks with me toward the bed, pumping his fingers in and out of me, a fierce look in his eyes, before he removes his fingers and lets me drop to the mattress.

I fall onto my back, bouncing a little at the force of him letting go so fast. He lifts moisture-coated fingers to his lips, and his tongue slips out as if to taste the essence I've left there.

"Mine." His eyes are dark pools, impossible to read.

I scoot backwards up the bed until I reach the headboard. He advances on his hands and knees toward me, his shoulder muscles and biceps rippling. How is he so buff? So fit when he must spend most of his time behind a desk? Firm hands push my thighs apart, and I expect him to slide between them and sink his cock deep inside me.

But he doesn't. Instead, he stills, staring down at my exposed pussy.

What is he thinking? Am I too wet? Not wet enough? Can he tell just from looking that I've hardly ever had sex? Does it excite him, that view, or is he repulsed?

I try to resist the urge to cover myself. I clench my fists as I grab at the bedcovers, but his continued scrutiny is my undoing. I creep one of my hands across and splay my fingers wide to hide my pussy from his view.

His brows draw together, and slowly, he shakes his head. "You are my wife now, Bianca. Don't do that."

"Fuck you." It isn't even a real challenge. I can't manage more than a whisper.

He smiles. "Yes. You will."

Then he takes the offending hand, removing it from my pussy and entwining his fingers with mine. He lifts my arm up above my head. I don't know why, or what he's doing, until...

Snap.

Something tightens around my wrist. It doesn't hurt, but when I pull, I can't lower my arm. I turn my head and gape at the built-in leather cuff in the headboard. How did I not know that those loops were more than decorative? While I pull at my hand, testing the strength of the loop that now encircles my wrist, he imprisons my other hand above my head too.

I shake my arms, glaring at him, arching my back up off the bed. My heart pounds as I consider all the things he could do to me right now.

I am helpless. At his mercy.

My insides clench, but not with terror. I hate my own body in this moment, even more than I hate Rio.

"Let me go." Staring into his dark eyes, I see no mercy. The last thing I want to do is beg, but I have to try. "Please?"

He kneels between my legs, preventing their closure, his hands relaxed on his thighs as he studies me.

"For the love of God, Rio. *Please*!"

"I will. But not yet. Do you know why, Bianca?"

I can't bring any more words. I shake my head.

"Because your pussy is dripping and swollen, and it tells me what you refuse to admit out loud."

He smirks down at me, but I barely notice. His cock is so hard and ready, and from this angle looks even bigger than it did before.

"You like being dominated more than you hate it."

Tears fill my eyes and overflow, falling down my temples into my hair. I shake my arms, testing the restraints again, but they hold firm. I open my mouth to plead with him to let me go, but something stays my voice.

Something dark inside, hidden deep, that rears up the moment I try to speak. I stop trying to squeeze my legs shut and instead let them widen, letting him see. He already knows, of course.

I do like it.

He will take me like this, and I will enjoy it. And then I will hate him all the more.

He nods as if he understands my inner battle.

Then he leans forward, looming right over me, one hand on each side of my ribs. "Why didn't you?"

"Why…" I swallow convulsively, and unease creeps in, overlaying the desire. This isn't in the risqué light bondage seduction script I just began playing in my head. "Why didn't I...*what*?"

He smiles at me, but there is no mirth in his expression. "You had the chance. Why didn't you simply bite off my cock?"

Rio

THE FEAR that flickers across her features is familiar. I am used to it from everyone around me at some point, and yet, in Bianca's golden-brown eyes, it seems wrong.

I'm not sure why.

I reach out and encircle her neck with one of my hands. Splayed, my fingers and palm easily cover the area beneath her jaw, and I squeeze lightly, enjoying the sensation of her involuntary swallow against my palm.

This is what I'm used to in my sexual partners. Dread and desire, intertwined. Their fear always wins, and that feeds my cruel side. My cock twitches, reminding me that my release with Bianca is long overdue.

I needed her from the moment I first laid eyes on her, trussed up on the floor of the hotel room.

Before that, even. When your beautiful eyes stared out at me from the photo that I gave to Danelli. From the moment I knew that we'd found you. And that you were destined either to die. Or to be mine.

I am about to knee her legs even wider, ready for my entry, when she lets out a shaky little breath.

"I wanted to," she says, the words vibrating against my palm. "God, how I wanted to."

She's so brave, my little bird. I have my hand wrapped around her neck, but still, she doesn't shy away from the truth.

"And you didn't, because…" I am genuinely curious.

I was ready for her to attempt it, of course, but she could have done significant damage if she'd wanted, before I pulled her off me.

"Because you trusted me not to," she whispers. "So, in the end, I didn't."

I frown, not understanding what she means by that.

If the situation were reversed, I would not have behaved as she did. With restraint.

I tighten my hand on her neck. Instead of the whimper I expect, she trills out a laugh.

"I still hate you," she says, and damn if her chin doesn't rise, giving me even easier access to squeeze her throat if I choose to.

Fuck. This woman. She throws me so far off-balance I don't know how to react.

I remove my hand from her neck and flex my fingers, rubbing my palm and still feeling the heat of her flesh on my skin.

A fresh wave of desire rolls over me so fast I don't have time to play with her. Instead, I simply grab her hips, line myself up at her entrance without any finesse whatsoever, and then thrust, hard. I slide in all the way until her channel grips me from the head of my engorged cock to the base.

She releases a half shriek. "Oh my fucking God!"

Fuck. She's so fucking tight. She said she wasn't a virgin. Was she lying? *Fuck.*

I can't control the urge to move, the need to feel her

muscles ripple around me as I pull almost all the way out and then pump in again. And again.

She begins to sob, but her body rocks beneath me, grinding up to meet me with as much force as I apply to her. "God, I fucking hate you. So fucking much."

"You hate *this*?" I thrust again, and she sobs harder.

"No. I hate *you*."

"You want this?"

"Yes. Oh my God, yes."

Her breasts are in my face, and I grab one and guide it into my mouth, sucking and biting at her nipple and drawing out almost uncontrollable moans from her throat.

Her taste, her scent, her *everything*, rises around me until there is nothing but her. And this.

I grab at her ass, keeping her in place as my thrusting movements ramp up. "If you tell me to, right now, I will stop, Bianca. And I will release you from those cuffs."

Her breathing rasps in the air, matching mine, as I continue to fuck her and wait for her response.

"Well?" I can't hold on much longer.

I need to come. Her channel clutches at me, and her whole body does this strange arching shudder.

Fuck, she's so damn fucking hot. I can't...

"Don't stop. Oh, God, *please* don't stop."

Her words and the accompanying cry tumble me over the edge, and I growl as I come inside her. She follows me only a second later, tight heat searing my flesh as the climax takes us both and her muscles clench in a frenzy around me.

I collapse onto her as our bodies still shudder and jerk. My chest heaves as I drag in breaths, then I roll to one side so I don't crush her. Somehow, I manage to reach up and release the cuffs.

I expect her to immediately launch off the bed, get as far away from me as she can. But she doesn't. She curls into my torso, her freed hands stroking my chest as her wayward hair gets in my eyes and my mouth. Her racing heart beating in time with mine is a strange comfort I can't explain.

For some reason, instead of pushing her away, I wrap my arms around her and stroke her back and hold her tightly. As if I never want to let her go.

Affection is an emotion I can't afford to show, and I'm certain I am about to pay for my moment of weakness.

14

"It's hard to hate someone once you understand them."
Lucy Christopher, *Stolen*

Bianca

IS THIS STOCKHOLM SYNDROME? I slept with my mob boss husband—the man who kidnapped me off the street and forced me to marry him. The man I keep saying I hate.

And yet, not only did I allow him to touch me—*fuck* me—I wanted him to do it. I wanted his hard, hot flesh embedded deeply inside me, with a desire crazier and more intense than anything I've ever felt.

What is wrong with me? I'm sick. I must be, to have allowed that. I must be, to want more of the same. More. Right now. Only, it's not going to happen, because I've woken up alone in the bed.

I rolled over to touch him, and there's nothing beneath the sheets but emptiness.

I thought I felt him in the night, his muscled arms surrounding me. I vaguely recall snuggling back into him, feeling his fingertips stroke down my back, hearing his soft laugh in my ear. A laugh that shifted my hair and tickled my neck.

Did I smile at that? Did I actually smile and make a contented moan as I pushed my ass back into his groin and thought about what we might do in the morning after we'd slept a little?

Fuck. I'm definitely sick. And this has to be Stockholm syndrome. There's no other explanation for this level of crazy pinging around in my head.

I lie in bed, thinking about Rio, wondering what it is about him that fascinates me and draws me into his orbit.

Because, no matter what he threatens—death, torture, destruction of the animal shelter and the careers of everyone who works there—there is nothing that could truly stop me saying no to him if I really wanted to.

There must be some small part of me that wants to be touched by a monster.

Is it because I'm from his world, even though I didn't know it until a few days ago? Is it innate in my blood? As a lost Mafia princess—a goddamn Carlotti if I'm to believe Rio —then maybe there's a darkness in my soul that recognizes him and his world as the place I truly belong.

No. I sit up, throw back the bedcovers, and stomp to the bathroom to shower. I don't accept that. I don't believe that. I wasn't like that for the previous twenty-five years of my life, and I refuse to reinvent my values and my moral code just because I'm confused about my desire for my kidnapper.

Even if he is now my husband.

Francine comes in with breakfast not long after I finish dressing. She gives me a side-eye when she sees what I'm wearing, but I don't care. I've chosen a pair of simple cream trousers and an olive-green top for comfort rather than glamour. They were in the dressing room, so I have to assume I'm allowed to wear them at some point. I've added slip-on flats and chosen not to wear makeup.

I have no idea if the wedding guests are all still here, or whether I'm supposed to be paraded around in front of them again, but if so, they can see me in normal clothes for once rather than an evening gown and heels.

I smile sweetly at Francine as I pour a coffee from the silver jug and then take a bite of toast. "What's on for today, then, Auntie?" I speak around the toast. "More hanging out in the suite here?"

"Well, I..." She scowls at me. "Francine will be fine. Aunt if you must. Auntie..." She screws up her nose, and I know exactly what I'll be calling her from now on. "I will double-check with Rio, but I believe you may be required out and about today."

I almost choke on my toast. I hadn't actually expected a positive response. Out and about means there may be opportunities to escape.

"Okay, that sounds...good." I leave off the "Auntie." I really do want out of here, and clearly, the only way to achieve that will be to behave. For now. "Thank you."

"You are welcome." She turns to leave, then pauses. "You really did make a beautiful bride, Bianca. You and Rio looked good together. I believe, in time, you will learn to be very happy with my nephew."

She seems genuine with a warmth in her eyes that is new.

I can't bring myself to respond in any way, except for a small nod that she notes before abruptly leaving.

This world. It is unlike anything I've ever known. I don't understand them at all. Most of the time, they seem cold and unfeeling, driven purely by vengeance or the need to build their endless wealth. And then out of the blue, I catch a faint glimpse here and there of what feels like humanity. In Francine just then, and in Rio last night when he wrapped his arms around me and held me as if he cared.

It unsettles me. I don't want them to be human. I don't want to see anything positive in this horrific situation. I need to focus on the truth—that Rio heads a cartel of murderous criminals who flout the law and kill people for a living. That he kidnapped me, shot my friends—or at least his men did—and he has held me captive ever since.

That is my new reality, and I need to remember it every second of every day for the time I have left here in this compound.

And for as long as he allows me to live.

Rio

I AM PLACING trust in Bianca today by letting her out of her suite. Of course, she won't be able to get away—at least not far. My security team will see to that. But she doesn't know how closely she'll be watched, and it will be interesting to see what she does when I allow the caged bird a little taste of freedom.

"Come, my darling wife." I watch her from my seat behind the desk and beckon her in as she continues to pause in the doorway of my office. "Meet your new brother-in-law, Nicky."

Bianca looks fresh and clean, younger than her twenty-five years with little makeup and her dark hair tumbling down her back. She hesitates a moment longer, scuffling one foot back and forth, and then her chin comes up and she walks into the room with a small smile.

"We sort of met at the wedding yesterday," she says. "But pleased to meet you officially, Nicky."

She thrusts out a hand, and my brother shoots me an amused grin before reaching forward to clasp her tiny hand in his much larger one. "Charmed, Bianca. Rio is a very lucky man to have you by his side."

He releases her hand quickly. He knows better than to try and hold on too long to something I have claimed as mine.

"Hmm." She shifts her gaze briefly to me, and the fire I read there instantly ignites my cock. "I'm sure luck has little to do with Rio's life. He's far too calculating and strategic to allow luck to play any part."

Nicky laughs, and I resist the urge to growl as he says, "You already know your husband well, then."

"No," she says, surprising Nicky as much as me. Once again, her eyes seek out mine. "I think my new husband has many complex layers, and I don't believe I know much of him at all."

Interesting observation. I study her intently, looking for any sign of the fearful little bird she was when my men brought her here. In only a few days, she has lost the timidity that ignites my natural need to control her. To crush her.

I'm not sure how I feel about that. I don't know any other way to be, other than to use my power to control everyone around me. Bianca's seemingly newfound confidence while in my presence challenges everything I know about her. And about myself.

I don't like it.

"Leave us, Nikolas." I bark out the command, wanting to be alone with my wife at least for a few minutes before our next engagement commences.

And wanting my brother gone because I cannot afford for anyone to sense any uncertainty in my manner.

Uncertainty in my position means loss of power. Loss of face. Possibly even death.

There must be something unrelenting in my tone because Nicky doesn't hesitate. He gives Bianca a quick finger wave and disappears out the door, closing it quietly behind him, but not before shooting me a quizzical look.

Bianca half sits against the back of one of my sofas flanking the fireplace, studying me with an impassive expression. But she wraps her arms around her middle in a telltale action.

I lift my brows as I realize her confidence is at least partly a front.

"So, what's the plan now, Rio?" she asks. "Do I need to be kept locked up in that suite all the time? Or do you need me to perform for the guests, presuming most of them are all still here? What do you want from me now that we're married?"

What do I want from my wife? "I want many things from you, Bianca. But we will start with something simple. There is a luncheon on the river today for those wedding guests still remaining.

"I want you to accompany me to the event—which will be held on my cruiser—and I want you to act as if you are enjoying your new life as my wife. There will be important people at the luncheon. People who need to see us present a united front. So, let us start with that, Bianca, and see how we go from there."

She pouts in a delightfully annoyed manner, and once again my cock stirs. Her mouth on my flesh last night was perfection. She had a hesitancy about her actions as she took me between her lips that spoke of innocence, but the sensations she elicited with that smooth up-and-down, suck-and-lick movement had me struggling to avoid coming right there down her throat.

Her tongue darts out to moisten her bottom lip, and I have to stop myself from rushing around the desk and crushing her mouth beneath mine.

"Well?"

She hasn't responded.

"Shall we try to act like man and wife, Bianca? Or will I call my men and have you placed back in the suite once again?"

"All right." Her voice is small and slightly husky. She clears her throat. "I'll do it." Then she sighs, and her arms drop to her sides. "I suppose you want me all dolled up again like a plastic mannequin?"

I tilt my head, unsure why there's a part of me that enjoys the faint acerbity in her tone. I would tolerate that from no one else—except possibly Nicky—and I can't pinpoint why I allow it from her.

"I think not," I say at last. "You are perfect as you are."

"Oh!"

I smile at her surprise. "You look young and innocent. They won't be expecting that."

Her shoulders slump. "Right. Of course."

Finally, I rise to my feet and come around from behind

my desk. She flinches a little as I reach her. She is confident, and yet not. That dichotomy, too, excites me. Everything about Bianca excites me.

"Are you going to behave today, little bird?"

"If it allows me some freedom, then yes," she says, lifting her chin and gazing boldly up into my face.

But there's a flicker of something deep behind her eyes. Resentment? Defiance?

The defiance excites me more than anything else.

Challenge me. I dare you, Bianca.

I grab her hips and drag her against me, wanting her to know my need. Hot, hard, and ready.

Her eyes widen and lips part. The defiance disappears, and in its place is raw, naked desire.

"Remember this moment, little wife," I say, leaning down and almost, but not quite, touching my mouth to hers. "I want you. Make no mistake. And I will have you again. Over and over. Until you scream for mercy and release in equal measure."

Her breath shortens, tiny pants erupting from her throat.

I shift a lock of hair back off her temple and stroke my fingertip down her cheek to her jawline.

"But first, I show you off to our guests. Mafia royalty are here today, and you are now a queen among them. Just be warned, whether or not you like that fact, you will act as if you do, or suffer the consequences."

15

"We are not trapped by our thoughts. What we generally do, however, is create thoughts that trap us."
Joshua David Stone

Bianca

I KEEP TELLING myself I'm cooperating with my kidnapper because that will give me the best opportunity to escape.

In this world, cooperation equals freedom, and I stand here on Rio's luxury cruiser on the river, doing my best to behave as he wishes. But I've had a lot of alone time lately with nothing to do but think—and overthink—everything. And there's more to my motives than a simple desire to gain my freedom from Rio Agosti.

As much as I hate who he is and what he stands for... As much as I want to get away and see him punished for what he did to me and to my friends...my damn traitorous body makes a mockery of my vengeful thoughts.

My body desires him with an intensity I never expected or thought possible, and that muddies the waters when it comes to making decisions about how and when to make a run for it.

I stare around the cruiser, filled with beautiful women and powerful men, lift my champagne goblet to my lips, and sip slowly. The French bubbly is expensive—the best money can buy, as is everything else on this boat—and the food being handed around by impeccably dressed waitstaff has been designed to tempt even the fussiest eater.

Not that I can eat anything. Not when my stomach is tied up in knots, and the acid churns so fiercely it feels like a hole is burning right through my insides.

The sun is warm on my shoulders and back, the afternoon shaping up to be one of the warmest of the season so far, and the buzz of conversation around me is full of happiness and satisfaction.

This is my post-wedding day lunch. *I'm* supposed to be happy too. In the real world, back where I came from only a short time ago, I would have been ecstatic if I had just gotten married and was hosting an afternoon party on the river in such a picturesque location.

In *this* world—the world of cartels and crime lords— happiness seems like a pipe dream.

I turn away from the crowd and stare down at the brown river water gently lapping at the cruiser's sides, contemplating the chances of survival were I to simply jump over the side and sink beneath the murky depths.

I was good at swimming at school. I can hold my breath longer than the average person. If the water is deep enough to hold this large boat and the several others currently berthing at Rio's riverfront property, then surely it would be deep enough that I could be carried unseen beneath the surface by the currents that eddy and swirl around us?

Where is Rio right now? And Francesca, and Nicky, and all the security people who've been keeping watch? I glance over my shoulder, and no one seems to be looking at me.

I could do it. I could slip over the side and be gone before they even know what happened. Would they shoot at the water if I did? Would it matter?

I am as good as dead anyway if I stay here. I can't see Rio wanting to keep me around for longer than it takes to show this cruel, glittering world that we are a couple. To demonstrate that he does, indeed, have control over the Carlotti fortune.

Once he's finished showing me off, and the official paperwork is signed, he will have no further need of me. And at that time, I will be expendable. Collateral damage in a deal that will cement him as the most powerful man in this region.

The conviction coalesces in my mind, and I carefully place my champagne flute on the tray of a passing waiter. Then I grip the deck railing so tightly my knuckles turn white.

Deep breath, over the side, kick off the shoes, and swim with the current beneath the surface until I can no longer hold my breath. Resurface, breathe, and then do it again. And again. Until I am as far from Rio as I can get.

I can do this. I *can*.

Then…why don't I?

Why do I simply stand here, gripping the top of the barrier as if I'm frozen in place? Why do I not…*move*…

I stare down at the water for one minute. Two.

Until the moment for escape passes, and a deep voice in my ear says, "Another champagne, little bird?"

I don't even look at him. I can't. He will either be gloating with a self-satisfied smirk, or he will be angry with that ice-cold rage more terrifying than the hot anger most people display when they're upset.

"Sure. Why not?" Why the ever-loving hell not? Perhaps I should get drunk.

I hold out my hand, and he slips a full glass into it. I thrust it up to my mouth and take a large sip. A gulp, almost.

"Steady," he says quietly. "There's a ways to go before this day finishes, Bianca."

I do look up then because there's a note in his voice I don't expect. Concern? It can't be.

But there it is, deep behind his eyes. Concern and curiosity. No gloating and no rage.

"Why did you not do it?" He's still speaking quietly.

"Why did I... Wait. You...*knew*?" How could he know what I'd been considering? What I'd almost done.

"Of course I knew. I was watching you from the upper deck." He lifts his chin, and I follow his gaze to where more people are mingling on the higher deck above us.

"And yet you didn't rush down here to stop me jumping? Or send your goons down to keep me in place?"

"If you run, you know what will happen. And there is nowhere you can hide from me, Bianca. I will always find you. So, I waited. I wanted to see if you would. I repeat my question. Why did you not jump over the side when you had the chance?"

I frown at him, trying to articulate my reason for not trying to escape, but in the end, I stick with the truth. "I don't know. I wanted to. I almost did, and then, I just didn't."

Not much of a response, but the brief quirk of his lips at one corner shows me he isn't too disappointed with my response. "Honesty. I like that in you, Bianca. Always be honest with me, and I will afford you the same in return."

"All right." I turn and face the water again, shivering as a light breeze suddenly kicks up, lifting my hair. "Are you going to kill me?"

A short chuckle is his answer.

I shoot a look up at him. "Honesty, Rio. Please."

He leans his forearms on the railing beside me, and I wait for what feels like forever before he opens his mouth as if to answer. But then he snaps it shut again when a group of men approaches us.

One of them is his brother Nicky. Another is Carlos Rossi, the man who said he knew—and loved—my mother. I have no idea who the others are. They were probably at our wedding, but everyone's faces were a blur yesterday.

"You can't hog the beautiful bride all afternoon, brother. How are you doing this afternoon, Bianca? Survived the wedding night with Rio, I see." Nicky lifts my free hand and plants a kiss on my knuckles, his lips lingering a second too long on my skin.

The gesture is strangely endearing, and an obvious challenge to Rio who seems to bristle beside me.

I resist the urge to roll my eyes at the testosterone display from both of them, instead shooting a tight smile of greeting at Nicky before snatching back my hand and turning to Rossi. "How are you today, Mr. Rossi? I trust you enjoyed our...wedding?"

My voice drips with sarcasm, and for some reason, all the men laugh as if I've said something highly entertaining.

"Please, my dear. Call me Carlos." He then looks at my

husband. "May I steal away your bride, for a few minutes at least? Not too far. Perhaps we might take a seat just over there."

He points toward a cushioned bench seat that offers a little shelter from the sun.

I open my mouth to agree, but Rio answers before I can get a word out. "You may. Five minutes, Rossi. There are others I wish her to meet."

Carlos smiles, but there is no mirth in his expression. "Of course. Come, my dear."

He crooks his arm, obviously expecting me to take it. When I do, he guides me over to the bench seat and then waits until I sit before he joins me.

"Next time, ask me directly," I say, trying to be polite but not hiding my annoyance. "You don't need to ask *him*."

He shakes his head. "It doesn't work that way in our world, Bianca."

"So, I'm Rio's…*possession* or something? Now that we're married? He…what? *Owns* me?"

"You are his, yes." Carlos nods calmly as if he's simply talking about the weather.

I am his.

I will never be his. And yet, in some ways, I know I already am.

I stare at Carlos, wondering how close he was to my parents. "So, if I asked you to help me get away from Rio…"

His eyes widen.

Desperation fills me as I read the "no" in his expression without him having to say it out loud. "For the sake of my mother?" I add. "You said you loved her. Didn't you? *Please*, Carlos."

My voice thickens as my throat clogs with sudden tears. Will I never get away from this place?

I should have jumped into the river when I had the chance.

You fool. You goddamn, bloody hesitating fool.

Carlos leans forward and briefly pats my knee. "I did love your mother, yes. You look so much like her, my dear. And for that reason, I wish to give you a little advice."

"Advice?" Somewhere along the way, I've lost the glass of champagne. I cross my arms over my chest to stop the nervous fidgeting that my fingers itch to do. "Okay, I'm listening."

"Rio will soon have you sign over your rights to the Carlotti empire. It is vast, Bianca, and as the sole remaining Carlotti, you are an extremely wealthy woman in your own right. Your father was a clever businessman and ran a tight crew back in the day."

A laugh threatens to bubble up and out of my clogged throat.

My father's *crew*? My father's *fucking crew*?

Carlos is still speaking. I blink away my impending hysteria and try to focus on his words.

"Sign the papers. Do whatever he asks of you. And when the time is right, I will step in and help you wrest it all back. But I have to warn you, my dear. Never try to run from Rio. His reach is far too powerful."

He pulls out a handkerchief and mops at his brow. I'm still processing his previous words about my father. My family. My *empire*.

"You fascinate him, at present," Carlos continues. "That much is obvious to all who see you together. But make no mistake, if you run, he will never forgive you. He will hunt you down, and he will kill you. And then he will kill everyone you've ever loved or held dear. It's who he is, Bianca. It is all he knows, and I do not want you to ever experience the terror of being on the wrong side of Gregorio Agosti."

16

"Marriage is the only war in which you sleep with the enemy."
Francois de La Rochefoucauld

Bianca

How do I stay on the right side—as Carlos Rossi put it—of Gregorio Agosti? Is it possible to avoid the metaphorical axe falling when I'm married to a mob boss? I'm never sure when or from what direction the next threat will appear.

I do little during the day except sit around in my suite while various people visit to provide expensive manicures, pedicures, facials, and hair treatments.

A woman arrives one morning with an entourage who wheel in rack after rack of clothing. I am invited to choose the pieces I want while the woman measures up every inch of my body so they can customize my choices.

The visit is terrifying for what it implies—a long-term future as Rio's wife, where I may actually need all these pieces of fancy clothing, and all I can think about is one day being able to escape and get back to my old life.

Except my old life is gone.

Nothing will ever be the same again, even if I do manage to get out of here and rejoin the team at Lots of Paws. Not that they'd have me back after what happened right on their doorstep.

The bigger issue is that I can't *unknow* what I know now —that I was born into a Mafia family; that my blood is tainted by the violence that touched my friends and threatened the people and workplace I care about.

There's no coming back from that.

Francine continues to deliver food in her usual deadpan manner, and every so often, I'm allowed out—accompanied, of course—into the estate gardens to stroll and get some fresh air.

In truth, I've never been more bored in my life. Is this how rich people fill their days? I've always studied or worked and looked after myself, and at the rescue center, things like manicures and perfectly coiffed hair are a total waste of time and money.

The nights, however, have become completely different from my days. The first two nights after the luncheon on the river, Rio left me completely alone. I should have been relieved, but instead found myself tossing and turning and wondering if he'd somehow stopped desiring me.

Why should I care if he doesn't want me any longer? I should be pleased about that. But for those two nights, I only managed to fall asleep somewhere near dawn, tangled in my silken sheets and wondering if Rio was in some other woman's bed. Buried deep inside her willing pussy and making her scream as she came, like he did to me.

The third night, the claustrophobia got to me. I left the bedroom curtains wide and threw open the doors that led onto the large balcony. When I lay in bed, at least I would have fresh air coming into the room and be able to watch the stars as I contemplated my current crazy existence.

As I turned from the window toward the bed, a shadow moved near the bedroom doorway. I let out a tiny scream and automatically jumped back, trying to hide my nakedness.

"Rio! You scared me!"

He stepped fully into the room, and the moonlight illuminated his features. He was unsmiling, as always, and I couldn't read the expression in his eyes as they remained in shadow.

He moved swiftly, coming around the bed and grabbing hold of one of my wrists in a tight grip.

Excitement pooled between my legs at his touch. At the slight roughness in his movements as he pulled me close.

At the gruffness in his tone as he announced, "I have had unexpected business the past two nights, but it is done. I want you, *cara mia*."

Cara mia? I didn't have time to process the phrase and its meaning before his mouth crushed against mine, and I was transported instantly into a state of need. Need for him. For his touch. My body had been craving it for days, and I hadn't known how much until that moment.

There was no foreplay that night beyond that first crushing kiss. When we broke off, both of us breathing heavily, he simply picked me up, threw me onto the bed, and then flipped me over onto my stomach.

While I gasped and scrabbled among the bedclothes,

trying to find my purchase with hands and knees, he unzipped his trousers and gripped my hips, dragging me back toward him and impaling himself deep inside me.

I yelped at the invasion, but it felt so bloody good that my yelp was followed by a decadent moan. I wriggled my ass, trying to force him even deeper, and then he began to thrust.

"Oh my God, Rio. Yes. More."

He growled above me. "Quiet, woman."

"No, I—"

The sting of a hard slap on my left butt cheek instantly stopped my words.

Instead, I just whimpered and silently begged for more by dropping my face right down onto the sheets to give him the best access possible.

He fucked me hard, and fast, and the rush of heat inside me as he came sent me over the edge into an orgasm of my own.

There was no finesse that night, only need. No tenderness, only release. Until he carried me to the bathroom, and we started all over again beneath the sting of a hot and steamy shower.

Now, Rio visits my bed every night and stays until almost dawn. As much as my anger and frustration about my imprisonment grows, so too does my desire for my husband.

I may be reluctant to admit it, but I cannot deny it any longer, either to him or to myself.

I am desperate for Rio's touch. And for some reason, he also seems desperate for mine.

WE HAVE HAD sex every night for the past two weeks. Amazing, toe-curling sex. I never knew it could be like this—the more you have it, the more you want it. Is it that way with everyone, or does it only feel like that because my body desires him so intensely?

The curtains remain wide open every night, and I've come to enjoy the experience of watching dawn creep in each morning. It is one of the few things I do love about my current situation, and I know I will likely sleep forever more with uncurtained windows—no matter what the future holds.

Seeing Rio sleep is one of the few times I feel like I'm seeing the real man beneath the rigid mask he wears in every waking moment. The constant hardness of his features softens slightly in sleep, his jaw is less set in granite, and I find myself gently tracing the contours of his face as I rest my cheek against his chest and listen to his slow and steady breathing.

The first time I touch his face, he instantly wakes and snatches my hand away so fast my heart skips a beat.

His gaze is hyperalert, wary, until he takes in the fact that it is only me trying to caress his jawline. After several seconds, he releases my wrist and settles back against the pillows, folding his arms behind his head.

"I don't sleep in front of others," he says bluntly.

"Except me." There's an unexpected surge of pride as I realize I'm one of the few he has allowed to peek behind the mask—even if he hadn't meant to allow it, or to fall asleep in front of me.

"It would seem so."

The faintest hint of vulnerability in his tone is so shocking I automatically reach out and run my fingers down his jaw

127

once again, wanting to comfort him. He stiffens, but this time allows the caress without stopping me.

Now when I touch him while he's sleeping, he shifts but doesn't fully wake. Occasionally, his usually cruel-looking mouth lifts at the corners in a faint smile.

Making Rio smile has become one of my favorite things in all this madness.

I have no idea what is happening between us. I still hate him—or at least, I hate who and what he is, and what he's done to me and no doubt to many others over the years—but he fascinates me in a way that no other man ever has.

Rio is a beautiful, fascinating monster, and I'm like a moth to the proverbial monster flame.

One morning, as Rio is about to slip out of my bed, the craziness of our situation explodes out of nowhere and fills my head and my heart.

I grab for his arm, not even sure what I'm doing or why. "Please, Rio."

The sun is cresting the horizon, and golden rays are beginning to tiptoe across the landscape outside. This time, he has stayed longer than usual, and his obvious reluctance to leave me each morning is perhaps what has emboldened me this time.

He stills at my plea, then his back muscles ripple as he straightens and swings his legs over the side of the bed. He looks at me over his shoulder, eyebrows raised quizzically.

"Please what?"

I sit up, drawing my knees toward my chest and clutching at the sheet to cover my naked breasts. "I can't live like this anymore!"

The words burst out of me, and his raised eyebrows lower into a scowl. His eyes darken, his displeasure momentarily obvious even in the shadows of the early morning light. Then the frightening "nothingness" that he displayed when I first knew him descends over his face.

I swallow hard. I hate that "nothing" look.

I'd almost forgotten about it because I haven't seen it for several days. It scares me more than his anger, that look, because it turns him back into a detached monster who can make life-and-death decisions without seeming to care about any consequences.

I squeeze the edges of the sheet in my clenched fists. I may be afraid, but for the sake of my sanity, I have to ask my next question.

"I'm not used to sitting around doing nothing, Rio. Having people pamper me. It's not my style. I need to *do* something with my life. A job, some form of contact with the outside world—a phone? Access to the internet? Even a newspaper would be a start. I'm going crazy from the boredom. From the disconnect with everything and everyone. Except you."

"Am I not enough for you?"

I open my mouth to lie and say "yes, of course you are," but the truth pops out instead. "No. You're not."

He blinks as if I've shocked him in some way.

"You asked me always to be honest with you."

"I did." He stills as if thinking before he adds, "You're asking for contact with the outside world."

At my nod, he studies me a moment longer, then rises and pulls on his clothing. There is no hurry in his actions; there rarely is. He is always in control, methodical, and emotionless, and right now appears to be no exception.

"We both know what will happen if I allow that," he says at last, when he's fully dressed.

He moves to the door and looks at me with an unreadable expression.

"I won't." I shake my head and can't seem to stop shaking it. "I promise. I won't run. If I promise on my life—and on the lives of my friends and work colleagues—not to run, will you please just give me *something*? Please!"

Eventually, he lifts one broad shoulder in a shrug. "I will consider it. There is a gala event tomorrow evening I am expected to attend…"

His eyes narrow as if he's considering and discarding the idea that I might attend alongside him. I try to make myself look as nonthreatening as possible, deliberately allowing the sheet to drop and expose my naked breasts. Subtly, I arch my back a little, pushing them forward into his view.

God, what has he turned me into?

His gaze drops to my exposed body, then abruptly he turns and leaves.

Well, so much for using sex to sell my message.

I flop back against the pillows, fighting the urge to scream my frustration out loud. Once again, I've been left to face the dawning of yet another day as Rio's wife. Alone.

And with no solution as to how to escape this crazy and intolerable situation.

"In the truest sense, freedom cannot be bestowed; it must be achieved."
Franklin D. Roosevelt

Bianca

LATER THAT MORNING, when Francine arrives with a pot of coffee and a blueberry muffin—I had mentioned to Rio one night that I love blueberries—there's a surprise waiting on the breakfast serving tray alongside the coffeepot and food.

A folded newspaper.

My first communication—of sorts—with the world outside this isolated compound.

I snatch it up before noting the date is from a week or so ago. My heart sinks. Old news it is, then. Though even that is better than nothing.

Francine must see my disappointment because she suddenly speaks up. "He thought you might like to see this edition in particular. Page five."

I dutifully open the paper to the page she indicates and can't help the gasp that escapes. There's a massive photo of Rio and me at our wedding. It looks to have been taken after the ceremony just as we exited the chapel. My arm is draped through the crook of his elbow, my hand resting on his forearm, and his other hand covers mine. He is staring down at me with the faintest hint of a quizzical smile on his lips.

Heat fills my cheeks as I study the besotted look I'm giving him in return. Even then, my desire for him must have been obvious to everyone around us. My desire, and a sort of fiery passion that could be interpreted a number of different ways by people who don't know me.

Anger. Impatience. Desperation to get through the festivities and take my new husband to bed. Any one of them could apply, even though *I* know it was rage at the circumstances that fueled my system that day.

God, I don't even look like *me* in this photo. I glance at my reflection in the mirror above the fireplace in the sitting area.

I don't look like the old me at all anymore.

I look like a Mafia wife. Polished and elegant and with an almost hidden passion burning just below the surface, darkening my eyes and lifting my chin in defiance.

Dismay kicks me in the gut as I realize everyone from my old life will likely have seen this photo and read the accompanying article that takes up most of the page. The journalist must have been primed by Rio's people. Of course he would have been. That's how it works in this world.

The article talks about my discovery of my true heritage,

and hints that Rio kindly helped me navigate the path to becoming Bianca Carlotti. It states that we instantly fell in love and into a whirlwind courtship that ended in our marriage. It concluded that the uniting of two great Boston-area families can only mean great things for this city and the region.

Fuck. Me.

I throw the newspaper into the fireplace, anger seething within me as I watch the paper burn.

No mention of the truth. Of the fact that he kidnapped me at gunpoint. That his goons *shot* my friends. That they hit me in the face, stuffed me in the trunk of a car, and that he *forced* me to marry him by threatening to hurt people I care about.

Has he forgotten all of that? Is he simply a psychopath who rewrites reality to suit his own warped version of the truth?

I haven't forgotten. And I never will.

Francine grunts and shakes her head as we both watch the newspaper burn. There is censure in her gaze when I turn away from the flames.

Too fucking bad. She's as awful as he is. I raise my chin and glare at her, daring her to say something about the article.

Instead, she says, "He wants you ready for a meeting at eleven. You have papers to sign, I believe. And then tonight, you will attend the gala on his arm. I argued against the latter, of course, but he insists."

"He's letting me out to the gala?" I gape at her, my mind spinning with the unexpected news. Then the other part of what she said penetrates. "Wait. Papers to sign? You mean…"

My heart skips a beat. So, I guess today's the day I sign over the Carlotti empire to Rio Agosti. Unless I dare to defy

him, of course. But if I do that, people I care about will probably end up dead.

IT IS DONE. The papers are signed, and Rio is now formally in
control of the Carlotti empire that I never even knew existed
until his men snatched me off the street and turned my entire
life upside down.

I raise my eyes to Rio's, ignoring the team of lawyers
around the conference table who are shuffling contracts and
paperwork back into their briefcases and making moves to
leave the office where I've just signed over my life.

"Are you happy now, *husband*?" I don't bother to hide the
bitterness in my tone.

It isn't that I want the money for myself. I would have no
idea what to do with such wealth, or how to head up a cartel.
And I don't want to touch anything that is most likely created
from blood. I have no idea exactly what my parents did to
build the Carlotti empire, but I can't imagine it was all clean
and legal.

Not in this industry. This *life*.

No. None of those things lace my voice with vitriol.

What really has my gut churning is the way Rio went
about securing my fortune as his. If my birth and heritage had
been explained to me in a civil and rational manner, and I'd
been allowed to make decisions for myself in relation to my
life and my future, I may have been able to make a positive
difference to so many people's lives.

When Rio kidnapped me, had my friends *shot*, and
destroyed everything I ever knew about my life—including
my very identity—he took away my ability to choose for

myself. And despite the fact that his presence turns me on sexually, I can't forgive him for removing the basic human right relating to choice.

There's also a tiny part of me—a part I'm trying to ignore —that dreads the moment he announces that he no longer needs me. He has my money. My name. And the rights to my family heritage, such as it is.

He doesn't need me anymore. I wonder if we'll get an annulment or a divorce?

Rio meets my gaze, and a shaft of dread spears through me at the lack of emotion in his features. Even after the physical closeness we've shared, he seems completely unmoved by anything except business.

What if he doesn't want a divorce? What if he simply has me killed? It would be far cheaper for him, I'm sure, to just put a bullet in my head and dump me with concrete boots in the river behind his estate.

As if he can sense the fear that ratchets up my pulse rate, Rio's mouth lifts at one corner. Yet there is no humor in that smile of his, only derision. He places his hands carefully on the conference tabletop, fingers splayed, and slowly rises to his feet.

"I am satisfied with the outcome of today's meeting." His gaze shutters even farther, and he turns away before casually swinging back as if he's only just remembered. "Tonight's gala is a test. Fail it, and there will be consequences. *Wife*."

His derisive grin widens, becoming wolfish, and then he's gone in a flurry of movement, leaving me with a roomful of lawyers and a bodyguard who indicates with an impassive air that I should precede him out the door.

Rio

IT GOES against everything in me to allow Bianca to attend the gala this evening. There will be more than four hundred and fifty guests, including covert law enforcement, I am certain, given the guest list. And the event, to be held at the Renaissance Waterfront, will be extensively covered by the media which adds yet another layer of complexity to keeping Bianca compliant.

There will be many opportunities for my wife to slip away from me or speak up publicly about how our marriage came about. She will regret it if she does.

Many of the media in attendance are on my payroll, and those who are not can no doubt be persuaded to write what suits me and my family.

Still, I brief Danelli carefully beforehand, ensuring he understands the importance of keeping eyes on Bianca at all times. Even if he has to double the usual security or pay the team a premium. Whatever it takes for them to do their job, and keep her from running, has my approval.

I meant what I said to her in the conference room earlier. If she gets through tonight and behaves herself, she may earn herself more freedom. If she does not, there will be consequences, and she will feel my wrath.

The frisson that runs down my spine as I wait for her at the estate's front entrance is not familiar to me, nor is the second-guessing going on in my head.

I do not second-guess. I know what I want, and I do what it takes to get it.

Control. And power. They go hand in hand. That's how I was raised, and how I keep my position at the head of this family.

Bianca has created a tiny crack in my innate self-confidence. I need to remedy that. Soon.

And yet, I can't seem to bring myself to get rid of her, even though we both know I no longer need her now that the Carlotti empire is officially aligned with mine.

Images spool in my mind. The way she glares at me with such hatred, and then her eyes darken and melt when I take her in my arms and claim her body. The way she rolls her bottom lip between her teeth when she's nervous, but sways her hips with quiet confidence when she moves. The way her scent rises around me, sending my senses into overdrive every time she's near. That tiny sound she makes when I thrust with my ready cock into her heated pussy—a cross between a moan and a whimper that sends an electrical charge straight to my groin.

Everything about Bianca is contradictory and intriguing. As if the woman she was raised to be—Bree—has been overlaid by her Carlotti blood, but Bree refuses to give up and disappear altogether.

She is both Bree and Bianca, all rolled into one, and somehow has carved a path deep into my thoughts without me even realizing when or how.

My cock stirs, as if just thinking about her has recreated her scent and her sounds and her compelling siren call. I shift from one foot to the other, tamping down the ill-timed need.

There will be time for that later. If she behaves. And if not, then my little wife may well find herself on the receiving end of a much-deserved spanking. Though, judging by her responses already, a spanking may well be less of a deterrent than I intend.

I glance at my watch—she is close to running late. I am

about to send someone up to check on her when I see movement at the top of the stairs.

She descends slowly in her heels as if she's a little afraid of falling, and it isn't until she reaches the bottom step that I realize I haven't taken a breath since she appeared.

I suck in air through my nose and then expel it, deep and slow. When I am finally back in complete control, I speak. "You look stunning, Bianca. Beautiful."

Her dress is long and sparkling silver. The fabric hugs her curves, leaving little to the imagination despite the modest cut of the neckline. At least, it is modest at the front. At the rear, which I notice when she turns slightly, the dress exposes most of her back.

Her hair is up for once, secured in a loose style with a diamond-studded clip, and her generous lips are coated in a deep ruby red.

She lifts her gaze to mine, searching my face as if trying to gauge my reaction. Pink suffuses her cheeks, making her even more beautiful, if that is possible. She glances down, then back up at me through her long dark lashes. Faux-innocent looks like that are where I can see both Bree and Bianca.

"Thank you, Rio. You..." She coughs and clears her throat. "You look very handsome, too, in your tux. As always."

I hold out my hand. She doesn't move, remaining still almost too long before finally stepping forward and linking our fingers together. I lead her out to the limousine waiting beneath the portico and hand her into the vehicle before climbing in after her. As the driver heads out of the estate toward the waterfront hotel, I keep Bianca's hand in mine, feeling a rush of something heady I haven't experienced before.

I stay quiet during the drive, spending most of the journey trying to identify what it is. It is not until we're pulling up to the hotel entrance that I finally work it out.

Alive. In Bianca's presence, I feel alive.

And that could be a major problem, because it means I have allowed her to get under my skin.

18

"There's a thin line between love and hate."
Simone Elkeles

Bianca

THERE WAS A MOMENT, as Rio watched me walk down the stairs at his estate, that I simply couldn't breathe. The molten heat in his gaze as he stared at me was so unexpected, I almost missed a step.

Luckily, I managed to regain control of my suddenly wobbly legs and reach the bottom without tumbling in a heap at his feet.

He is so handsome, in a dark and brooding way, though I don't believe he knows or cares about his own looks. The black tuxedo with white shirt and black tie is traditional fare, but on Rio, with his wide shoulders and powerful persona, the look transforms into stunning.

When he held out his hand, I froze. It felt like a pivotal moment in whatever this *thing* is between us. He is my kidnapper, my jailer, my husband, and now my lover. And my feelings for him remain a big ball of confusion in my chest.

It felt like a commitment, of sorts, when I stepped forward and linked my hand with his.

Commitment to see the night through on his terms, and to acknowledge the tiny bit of trust he is offering without attempting to run.

The gala is in full swing when we arrive. Hundreds of guests are milling around in the vast Pacific Grand ballroom space, sipping drinks and nibbling on canapes delivered by an army of servers. I had no idea before arriving what the event was for, but looking around at the décor and signage, I realize it must be for a hospital charity.

I start to worry at my bottom lip with my teeth, nerves getting the better of me, but then I remember that I'm wearing lipstick, and I surreptitiously swipe at my teeth with my tongue, hoping they're now lipstick-free.

How many here are involved in crime? Does the hospital and its board members know where some of their fundraising money likely comes from?

Before I can chase those thoughts any further, Rio slips an arm around my middle and holds me tightly to his side. His fingertips graze the edge of my breast, and I suck in a quick breath at the rippling sensation that fans out from his touch.

He leans down to whisper in my ear, "I like that I can switch you on that fast, Bianca. With only the tips of my fingers. It pleases me."

I stare up at him, and the look in his eyes morphs my inner tension into instant desire. I wish we were back in my bedroom—in my bed—before I realize that he has stopped us at the perfect spot for the milling photographers to get a shot of our entry. Right when I'm gazing up at him with what probably looks like adoration.

Again.

Cameras are everywhere, snapping in quick succession as he turns us slightly and nods at some of the photographers. Eventually, we move farther into the room.

"Well done," I mutter. "Very calculated."

"Of course. I want everyone to see that we are united as a couple tonight," he says. "Though I will not be by your side all evening. I have business to attend to."

"Business? Of course you do." My tone is dry, but I dutifully smile at one of the lingering photographers as they snap yet another final shot of the "happy" recently wed couple.

"I will never be far away from you, Bianca."

"You, or your kill team?"

He doesn't flinch at my attempt to get a rise.

"Don't worry, Rio, I know what you expect of me tonight. I'll behave."

"See that you do."

He stops a passing server, snags two fluted glasses filled with sparkling wine, hands me one, and takes a sip of his own.

His eyes meet mine over the rim, and my stomach churns.

I lift my glass and take a huge, fortifying gulp. "Will there be anyone I know here this evening? Do you expect me to make conversation with anyone in particular, or should I just wander and be seen? What do you need me to do, Rio? Why have you brought me here?"

I'm under no illusions. Rio wants me here for his purposes, not mine. My plea for something more than imprisonment at his estate probably just came at an opportune time.

"You won't be alone for long. People will flock to you. They will want to meet you—talk with you—because everyone is curious about the new Mrs. Bianca Agosti. If they ask how we met, be vague. Tell them our families have known each other for years. That, after all, is essentially true."

He lifts one of my hands and dusts a light kiss over the knuckles in a gesture that feels staged. "I will be back later to claim a dance from you, Bianca."

I resist the urge to snatch back my hand, and instead, I narrow my eyes at him. "Off you go, then," I manage. "Better not keep your *business* colleagues waiting."

His lips mash into a thin line. "Keep up the attitude, and you will pay for that later, my dear wife. In the bedroom."

"Oh, goody." I keep my tone light and slightly sarcastic, but I can't deny the shard of desire that shoots through me at the thought of what his bedroom punishment may entail.

Moments later, Rio disappears, swallowed up by the crowd, and I am left alone for what feels like the first time since this monstrous whirlwind began outside the Lots of Paws Rescue Center all those weeks ago.

Of course, I'm not really alone. There are several of Rio's goons dotted throughout the room, including the one who heads up his security team. His second-in-charge, Francine told me.

Danelli meets my searching gaze with his usual deadpan look. He too is dressed in a tux like Rio, darkly handsome and faintly dangerous-looking. But he is nowhere near as powerfully sexy as his boss. It seems my husband is the only one in the room who can instill desire in me with merely a slanted look or a delicate touch of his fingertips against my skin.

Rio's second lifts his glass in a mocking salute, and I turn away from him in a deliberate dismissal and begin to meander, scanning the crowd to see if there is anyone I may know. Unlikely, as these are not the type of people with whom I ever mingled as Bree Walker.

But if there's someone—anyone—who knew me before, maybe I can get a surreptitious message out to explain a little of what happened and somehow detangle myself from this mess.

A light hand on my elbow stops me only a few seconds into my exploration of the room. "Hello there. You look beautiful this evening, my dear. So much like your mother."

Carlos Rossi smiles at me with his twinkling eyes that somehow hide the truth of the monster I know must lie within. They are all so good at it—putting on the mask of civility.

The two security guards flanking him are carrying, and they are not as good at hiding it as Rio's men. Or perhaps it's just that their suits are not so expensive, and the cut of their jackets doesn't completely hide the bulge of their guns.

"Hello, Carlos. Fancy seeing you here."

He laughs at my wry tone. "Indeed. Everyone who is anyone is here this evening, my dear. There will be much interest in you, I am sure. Can you feel the eyes of the crowd upon you yet?"

His quip causes me to glance around uneasily. Is everyone truly watching me?

Oh God. Some of them actually *are*.

I notice one man in particular, staring more intently than the others. He is standing off to one side of the room next to a blonde-haired woman in a long red dress. I feel vaguely uncomfortable under the scrutiny, but when I meet his gaze, he turns and says something to the woman, and they wander off together toward the dance floor.

False alarm. I must have been mistaken about the man's interest. I guess.

I turn back to Rossi, frowning. "Are you here for Rio's business meeting too?"

His gaze sharpens, and unease fills me. Have I just inadvertently given away something I shouldn't have? *Oops*.

"Business meeting?" he says. "I was not aware one was scheduled for tonight. Who is in attendance, if I may ask? Other than young Gregorio, of course."

"No idea. This is the first time I've been allowed out of Rio's estate." I can't help the slight bitterness that coats my tone. "There is no way he'd let me in on any of his business dealings." Then I realize how that may sound. As if I *want* to get involved. "Not that I *want* to, mind you," I add quickly.

Rossi studies me for several seconds. I can't tell what he's thinking. But suddenly, the twinkly eyed uncle persona seems far away, and the calculating and possibly violent crime boss appears very close to the surface.

My breath shortens as visions from all the Mafia movies I've ever seen flash through my mind. The quick-fire turn from civility into violence. The way ordinary people are going about their ordinary business, and then suddenly they are gunned down in a sea of blood and gore.

Like Dave and Shelley.

Though that was on Rio's orders, not Carlos Rossi, but still... Same world. Same potential for danger.

I clutch tightly at my champagne glass and swallow hard.

"I believe you are telling the truth," he says at last. "You are not so interested in stepping into the family's shoes after all."

"Uh-huh. Yep. I mean, nope. I'm not." I nod like an idiot, and keep nodding, even as he takes his leave.

"It was lovely to see you, Bianca. We will meet again soon, I am certain."

"Sure. Great."

Carlos melts away into the crowd, and finally I can breathe properly once again.

As I turn away and take a couple of shaky steps in the opposite direction from Rossi, I notice again the couple who were staring at me earlier. They are still on the dance floor, swirling and twirling like others around them, but there is something about them that raises my hackles.

The woman's dress is strapless and figure-hugging, her hair swept up into a neat chignon. He is in the obligatory tux, and on the surface, they fit in perfectly with this crowd. But there is something watchful in their expressions as they look past rather than at each other. And his hand on the curve of her back seems...well, brotherly rather than intimate.

I wonder what it will be like when Rio takes me in his arms for the requested dance. *If* he does. Especially after he finds out I accidentally let slip about his meeting.

One thing's for sure—there will be nothing brotherly about Rio's embrace.

My husband was correct in one thing. I am inundated with people coming up to introduce themselves. It seems everyone wants a piece of the famous Mafia businessman's wife. Or at least, they want to satisfy their curiosity about what it was that drew him to me in the first place.

My money, I want to scream at them, over and over. My name. My family's empire. And now he has it all, and I have no idea if—or rather, when—he will decide to discard me by the wayside.

Instead of screaming, I smile and nod and murmur polite responses to the various questions everyone fires at me. How did we meet? How long have I known him? Was it a whirl-wind courtship? When was the moment I realized I was in love with the infamous Rio Agosti? Am I aware he is a suspect in a number of serious crimes?

That last couple of questions were asked by an older couple who clearly aren't on Rio's payroll. A headache clutches at my temples, and I stifle a groan. I need to get away. I need space.

I need my old life back again.

I murmur an indistinct apology and hurry away toward the powder room. When the door shuts behind me and I scan the anteroom and find it empty, I heave a sigh of relief.

Thank God. I need a few minutes to catch my breath. I cross to the farthest mirror and take a seat at the cushioned chair, positioned for those who wish to touch up their hair and makeup. I simply sit here, staring at my reflection and wondering who the hell is staring back at me.

Bree Walker is gone. I have to face that fact at last. There is nothing of the innocent, young girl left, except perhaps tucked deep down inside of me. I am Bianca Carlotti—for now, Bianca Carlotti-Agosti—and I have to figure out who that is and how I can find my new normal moving forward.

I drop my head into my hands and groan aloud, staying like that until I hear the whisper of the outer door opening.

When I raise my head, I meet the calculating gaze of the blonde-haired woman in the strapless red dress.

19

"Revenge is a dish best served cold."
Eugene Sue

Bianca

"Hello." The woman shoots me a small, tight smile, then strides across to take the seat beside mine. She throws her clutch purse onto the counter in front of her. "I'm Felicity."

"Hey." I don't give her my name in return, feeling wary.

Who is she, and what does she want?

She smiles wryly, as if she expected nothing else from me but my silent stare. "We don't have much time, Bree."

I start violently at her use of my old name—a name that seconds ago I was lamenting the loss of—but she is already glancing around as if to ensure we're alone and misses my shocked reaction.

"I work for a federal agency. We know what happened to

you, and we need your help to bring down your new husband, Gregorio Agosti."

I gape at Felicity, if that's her real name, trying to process what she's saying. A federal agency. Does she mean the FBI?

"There were witnesses, of course, to your kidnapping, but until you surfaced in the media as Gregorio Agosti's bride, we weren't one hundred percent sure who'd taken you."

"I...um..." *Witnesses*? I lean forward and clutch at her upper arm. "Dave and Shelley. My friends who were there... Are they..."

I can't even put the query into words. Hot tears of worry burn my eyes, and I furiously blink them back. What if Rio lied to me when he said they survived? What if they're both actually dead?

Felicity pats my fingers before shifting her arm out of my grip. "They're fine. Well, your friend Shelley is fine. They shot over her head, most likely to scare her back from the vehicle, I'd say. David Trentham apparently lunged at them, trying to get to you. They shot him in the left thigh. He'll be fine, eventually. I understand he's out of hospital and recuperating at home."

Oh, thank God. They're okay. They're really okay.

I hadn't realized I'd been carrying so much worry about them until this moment. I sag back in my chair. At least Rio told me the truth about that.

Felicity's mouth thins. "Neither of them is talking. We believe Rio got to them somehow. Either a threat or a bribe. But with your help..."

She reaches inside her clutch, pulls out a small, plain white card, and flicks it onto the counter in front of me. "Take it. My number is on there, as is my partner's. Call either one of us, twenty-four seven, and we will extract you, Bree."

Extract me? "What does that mean exactly?"

"We can put you into a witness program. Protect you from him, and then when you testify about what he did to you—"

"*Testify*? Whoa, hold on a minute. I haven't agreed to that."

He'd kill me. He'd kill my friends. My colleagues. He'd destroy everyone and everything I once knew if I betray him like that.

Even though everything in me is screaming out to be rescued from this terrible situation with Rio, the suddenness of this woman's approach is something I don't quite know how to process. I don't know her from Adam. She hasn't said which federal agency, if she even works for one at all.

"Do you work for the FBI?"

A short laugh releases from her ruby lips. "No."

"Which federal agency, then? Who the hell are you?"

Felicity stares at me without blinking. "Help us, Bree, and we'll help you. It's a win-win for everyone. Except that criminal Agosti."

It *does* make sense for me to testify against Rio for kidnapping me. He did the deed, after all. He may not have ordered his men to shoot Dave, but the reality is they did.

This moment, right now, I have the chance to open my mouth and agree to what Felicity is asking of me.

My mind skitters. *Just say yes. Just say yes. Say it.*

Somehow, I can't.

A win-win for everyone but Rio.

It's like that moment on Rio's boat on the river when I stared down into the murky brown waters. Why didn't I throw myself off the boat that day and sink below the surface with at least a partial chance to get away? To escape.

I didn't then, and I still don't know why exactly.

"He'd go to prison?" If I betray him. If I testify.

"On your testimony? I'm sure he would. Once you speak up, the others will, too."

"And you'd what? Put me into witness protection?"

"Yes, like I said." Felicity's tone is impatient, and she glances around again. "We're taking too long. We both need to get back out there, Bree, and—"

"Please don't call me that."

She frowns as if confused. "What? *Bree*?"

"My name is Bianca. Apparently. Not Bree. Even though I never knew that until recently."

"Well. Okay. *Bianca*." She jumps to her feet. "Think about it. Call us. We'll be waiting."

As she exits the powder room, I stare down at the white card in front of me. Slowly, I pick it up, considering what to do. I fold it in half, and then in half again. Then finally, I tuck it into my shoe. When I head toward the door, I have the strangest feeling that a brand is being burned into the base of my foot.

And if anyone looks closely enough, they'll see that the brand clearly states: *betrayal*.

Rio

DANELLI SAID she entered the bathroom over ten minutes ago. What the fuck is she doing? There are no exit windows, so I know she can't have escaped, but what if someone in there has hurt her? I should have insisted Danelli roster on at least one female to the security detail. I will ensure he does so in the future.

I open my mouth to order him to go in and check on her when the door opens. A blonde-haired woman in red saunters out and heads across to a waiting male. She greets him with a kiss, and they link hands and wander off.

My gut stirs. Something isn't right. I trust my instinct implicitly.

"Follow me in. Now!" I shoot the command over my shoulder, but I'm already heading in without waiting for my second to follow.

As I barrel through the door, I almost collide with Bianca who is in the act of reaching out for the door handle.

"*Fuck*!" I swivel, just avoiding knocking into her, then I grab her by the arms. "What the hell took you so long? I thought…"

I break off, hating that my voice and demeanor show anything other than calm control.

Her mouth parts as she stares up at me with wide, scared-looking eyes. Her cheeks are pale, and she looks…petrified, for want of a better word.

"Are you all right?" I bark out. "What's happened?"

"Nothing's happened. Other than you scaring the heck out of me. Why would you think something's happened?" She clutches her purse tight. "I felt a little unwell. Perhaps from the wine? I just needed a few minutes without everyone and their dog coming up and asking me about *you*."

"Right." I narrow my eyes. "Including Carlos Rossi, I hear."

"Oh." At least her pallor decreases when her cheeks pinken slightly. "Yes. I'm sorry about that. If something is meant to be a secret, you should probably let me know that in the future."

"No harm done. He arrived too late to have any impact on the outcome."

I hold the door for her, and we reenter the ballroom.

"The outcome of what?" Her hands clench on that purse; she seems to be using it like a shield. "I mean, sorry, it's none of my business."

For some reason, her thinly disguised curiosity amuses rather than annoys me. I decide to allow her a bit of slack. "Revenge is a dish best served cold, they say. I have received confirmation of something I have long suspected in relation to Carlos Rossi and his men, and I have arranged a little quid pro quo."

She stops dead. "But…are you saying you're going to…*kill* him in retaliation for something he did to you?"

"I did not use that word, little one. You do not need to know more. Except to be aware that Rossi, like all of us in this world of ours, knows the consequence of going up against the Agosti family."

She recoils slightly, and I decide to soften my words with a touch of humor. "Besides, he did not want me to win the bet we had in play. He is a sore loser, it would seem."

"You mean the bet over *me*? My name. My family's money." Her voice flattens all of a sudden, not hesitant or horrified as she was moments ago. Her fingers whiten as she clutches at her purse.

My gut is telling me again that something is up.

I nod at Danelli who steps forward. "Search her purse."

"Yes, Boss."

"Wait, no, I…" She tries to draw back, but Danelli easily removes the purse from her reluctant fingers.

He makes quick work of the search, then hands it back and shakes his head.

Nothing untoward.

"Does your man get off on studying my lipstick and tampons now?"

I ignore her childish taunt and hold out my hand. "You owe me a dance, Bianca. Presuming you feel up to it?"

"Why wouldn't I be up to it?"

I raise my brows. "You said you felt unwell. And there is a tone in your voice. Slightly antagonistic."

"Well, you know how it is. Talk of hits and death. *Searching* me. But my feeling unwell was temporary. I'm fine now. Let's dance, Rio."

She places her hand in mine and allows me to lead her out onto the dance floor, but when I take her in my arms, she is stiff and unresponsive.

"Relax," I command as the music changes to a slower beat. Her scent wafts up and wraps itself around me, and I tighten my hold, shaking her a little when she remains impassive. "I've a good mind to put you over my knee, little bird."

After a moment, whatever tension is holding her rigid begins to ease.

"Promise?" Her tone has become seductive now rather than belligerent.

She seems to be over whatever strange mood she was in minutes earlier.

"If you want it, then it isn't true punishment."

"I guess not." We circle the floor in silence, and then she speaks again. "You haven't called me that much lately."

"What? Little bird? Do you dislike the term?"

She shakes her head. "I should hate it. What it means; what it stands for. A caged bird. Trapped."

"But you don't hate it?"

She huffs out a breath. "I want to, but no. I don't. There's something in the way you say it…"

"Really, little bird?"

This time, she shivers and presses her body more firmly against me. "Yes. Really."

I allow my hand to wander down from her waist to her hip. She is tiny, but so curvy and feminine. "Then I will say it more often."

I trail my fingers around the edge of her dress, enjoying the goose bumps that rise up along her skin. The back of her dress is so low I can feel where the curve of her butt cheeks begins.

I tap her lightly there, enjoying the tiny mewl of sound that escapes her lips. I lean in and take her earlobe briefly in my teeth, pulling gently. "You are a witch, little bird. Drawing me in with your magic. And yet, you have been very good tonight. I am pleased with you."

The music rises, and conversation ceases as I succumb to the feel of my beautiful wife in my arms. I know Danelli and the team are keeping watch around us, and for a few minutes, I allow myself to simply *feel*.

She is changing me, this woman, in subtle ways, and I am not sure whether or not it is for the better. I have less focus, less control, when I am around her. I will have to put up my guard again. Soon.

For now, at least until this song concludes, I will hold Bianca and allow something softer to enter my consciousness.

But I will not forget that instinctive message my gut was trying to tell me earlier when she was in the bathroom.

Something is off. Something bad is coming.

Whether that instinct relates specifically to my wife, or to a less obvious threat, remains to be seen.

20

"Forgive yourself for loving the wrong person."
Unknown

Bianca

I THINK Rio is putting out a hit on another man because of a bet they made. Over *me*.

Nausea roils in my gut as he twirls me on the dance floor. I don't know how to let go of the guilt from such a thing. Is that what he meant when he mentioned the quid pro quo in relation to Rossi? What if he succeeds? What if he ends up killing someone because of *me*?

I was feigning illness earlier to get over the shock of seeing Rio only seconds after I tucked that little white card into my shoe. Now, the illness churning in my gut is real. But I can't do anything about it. At least tonight. It's too late to call Felicity back and tell her *yes*. I want help. I want to get away from this madness.

This life defined by violence.

And yet, as Rio continues to hold and guide me around the floor, my body begins to relax, as if my physical self and my mind are two separate entities. One can't seem to get enough of him. The other is repelled by who and what he is.

That term—little bird—started as a derogatory and controlling phrase. I know that. I am the one in the cage, and he holds the key. Now, there is something more when he says it, as if the door to the cage has been opened, and he is trying to entice me out.

Something has shifted between us.

Is that why I didn't speak up with Felicity? Will I find the strength to do so in the future?

Emotions swirl within me, exacerbating my nausea. Self-doubt, confusion, fear, and desire are all rolled up into one horrible, seething ball of tension. And yet through the tension, I realize I don't want Rio to let me go.

His arms are firm around me; his scent is almost comforting. Which is ridiculous given who and what he is. I should be disgusted with myself for letting such a man touch me; hold me. Affect me the way he does. I *am* disgusted.

But when he looks at me now, unlike when we first met, there is something real in his gaze. It is as if he finally sees me—the real me, and there are flashes of emotion in his expression now that were never there before.

Have I truly touched him in a positive way? Or is that merely my imagination trying to make sense of a horrific situation and finding mutual desire and need where none really exists?

"Sometimes your face is an open book, but at other times, I have no idea what you're thinking, Bianca. You hide from me. Like right this minute…"

He moves a hand off my hip and up to my face, caressing my jawline before forcing up my chin with one of his fingers. "What is going through your mind right now?"

I stare up at him, into his eyes, and think I see a hint of passion deep within his gaze. "I'm wondering if I'll ever see the real you, Rio. If you'll ever fully let me in."

I don't know why I say that. I know it probably isn't what he wants or expects to hear, but in this moment, I don't seem able to utter anything but truth.

His mouth curves up, just for a second, but any flash of humor is so rare that it seems super-meaningful coming from Rio. "I never let anyone in, Bianca. It is how I have achieved my position, and how I remain at the top."

Another twirl, and then he leans down to whisper in my ear, "But you do intrigue me. Far more than I ever expected, little bird. And there is something about you that draws me in, whether I want it to or not."

The nausea in my belly recedes, overtaken by sudden butterflies as my stomach flip-flops and settles into desire.

As if he can sense my need, his grip on me tightens. "Time to head home, my wife. I am going to make you scream before the night is done."

"Yes, please. Take me home, Rio. I want you to make me scream.""

I will think about Carlos Rossi tomorrow. About Felicity and the shadowy federal agency she may or may not work for. About hits and violence and stolen empires.

And crippling self-disgust.

Rio

BIANCA SAYS the word *home* in relation to my riverside estate, and it almost undoes me. I thread my fingers through hers and stride off the dance floor, pulling her along behind me.

I signal to Danelli with a sharp nod, and he taps his earpiece before speaking surreptitiously into the mic, presumably telling someone from the team to have the car brought round to the entrance.

Make me scream, she said. I cannot wait to oblige.

Bianca is like no other woman I have ever known. She is neither innocent nor experienced. She is both—and neither. I cannot categorize this woman in my head.

Except to know that I cannot seem to get enough of her. And in that fact, she may well be my undoing at some point in the future.

By the time we reach the hotel entrance and the security team advises it is safe to step outside, the limo is waiting for us. The driver holds the door, and I hand Bianca in then slide in after her. When the driver climbs into his seat, I order him to keep driving until I tell him to stop, and then I close the screen, affording privacy in the rear for Bianca and myself.

"Drive where?" Bianca asks curiously, her tone slightly breathless. "Are we not heading back to your estate?"

"Come here." I pull her across the seat and lift her onto my lap in a position that forces her beautiful dress to ride up her legs and bunch around her middle, exposing the smooth skin of her thighs.

"Oh! I… You feel…"

Her little moue of shock at my already-hardening cock now pressing at her core is an invitation I cannot ignore. I capture her mouth in a kiss, and she instantly releases a tiny sound and begins to kiss me back.

I grab her hips and knead her rounded ass, pulling her mound into me as her body rocks slightly back and forth. She is doing that just right. *Just. Fucking. Right.*

I break off our kiss to let out a small chuckle. "You learn fast." My voice is hoarse, rough.

"God, that feels good, Rio. So good. You're so hard, and ready…"

"*You* do that to me, little bird. With a look, a touch, or even that mewling sound from your throat when I claim you with my kisses."

"Do you mean like this?" Bianca leans forward this time to claim my lips, and when I slide my tongue into her mouth to taste her heat, a tiny whimper erupts from her throat and loses itself in mine.

Oh, little witch, just *like that.*

I lift a hand to palm one of her breasts through the silver dress, enjoying the swell that fits nicely in my palm, while I slide the fingertips of my other hand up her thigh to flutter across the scrap of lace covering her sex.

Even through the fabric, I feel her heat and her wetness. She is ready for me, so ready, and all we've done is kiss.

The scent of her need rises up around me, and my cock swells fully. I need to be inside her.

I curve my fingers beneath her panties and slip into her seam, swiping through the dampness as she breaks off our kiss and leans away slightly to allow me better access to her core. Her head drops back, and I reach up with my other hand to grasp and remove the diamond-jeweled clip that holds up her hair.

The dark mass tumbles down her back, brushing against my skin as I slip the thin straps of her dress off her shoulders. The fabric falls away, exposing her beautiful breasts.

The nipples are rosy-pink, taut and ready for suckling. I flick them with a finger, one after the other. "These are mine."

"Yes. All yours." Her voice is breathy, her eyes closed.

I take a moment to study her features—the delicate bone structure, her wide lips slightly parted, her freckles that even with full makeup still manage to peek through.

Everything about Bianca proclaims both innocence and allure.

Everything about her is different, new. Exciting.

Quickly, I unfasten my trousers, then grasp her hips and lift her up, positioning her channel entrance at the head of my cock.

Her eyes flash open, those golden-brown depths not alight with anger for once. This time, only arousal stares back at me.

"Now, fuck me, little bird. Hard. And don't stop until I give you permission to do so."

Bianca

I SINK DOWN onto Rio's hard flesh, and it feels so damn *right*. He fills me, deep and aching, and for a moment, I can't even move because I don't want to destroy the exquisite sensation of becoming one with another being. Becoming one…with *him*.

Then his fingers tighten on my ass, urging me into movement, and I can't maintain the stillness any longer. He thrusts beneath me, jolting me upward, and I begin to move, trying to meet him thrust for thrust as I rock back and forth and grind hard against him.

His hands are everywhere, on my hips, my ass, then up to my breasts as he grabs and kneads at my flesh. He dips his head and takes one of my peaked nipples into his mouth, sucking it in so strongly that desire mixes with pain.

I love it. There is no gap between the two. Pain and pleasure. They intermingle, and I move faster, more violently, as he pumps harder into me.

"Oh, God, Rio. It hurts, but it feels so good. So fucking good…"

His breathing is as torn up as mine. I love that I have that effect on him. That we affect each other in the same crazy way.

"Come for me, Bianca. Come for me. *Right now.*"

His command sends me over the edge into orgasm, and I begin to buck and cry out. Then heat burns inside me as he groans and releases his seed, and the moment tips into something more. Something so intense I cannot even describe it.

A scream erupts as everything I've been holding tightly within me shatters and falls apart. The sound reverberates around the confined space of the limousine, on and on. I can't stop it—I can't stop screaming… It is like my climax has opened the floodgates, and I just can't *stop…*

His mouth crushes mine, taking my sound into him, silencing me with his lips and teeth and tongue. Eventually, the sensations within my body begin to subside, and I fall forward onto his chest, allowing my head to nestle into the crook of his shoulder. Listening to his and my own ragged breaths finally begin to calm.

We stay like that for several minutes. He is still embedded inside me, but even as I realize that, he slides out and shifts me off his lap onto the seat beside him. We spend a couple of minutes straightening our clothing, and then I turn away from him, unaccountably embarrassed.

My reaction was way over the top. And yet, I could no more stop those screams erupting out of me than I could stop…well…breathing.

His fingers graze my back, just briefly, as if he wants to provide comfort but doesn't know how. Then his hand drops away, and he leans forward to rap on the dividing window.

When it rolls down, I keep my gaze averted, hoping the driver couldn't see or hear what was going on behind him. Knowing what is likely happening, and seeing or hearing it directly, are two different levels of awkward.

"Take us to the estate."

"Immediately, sir."

The window rolls up again, and we are once more enclosed in this small cocoon. A cocoon that now smells like sex and satisfaction.

"I made you scream."

I let out a huff of laughter at the smugness in his tone. "Yes, indeed you did." I can't resist a glance up at him. "It was too much, I know."

A single shake of his head surprises me. "No. I like the sound of your screams. I want more of that, Bianca."

"Oh." I sit quietly for a moment, digesting that. Then I say truthfully, "Me too, Rio. Much more."

Even as I say the words, Felicity's voice echoes in my head.

We need you to testify against your husband. We'll be waiting for your call.

I can't help but wonder if any future screams of mine will be induced only by desire. If I get on Rio's wrong side, they may well be induced by something so much more terrifying than making love with a mob boss.

21

"Who you were, who you are, and who you will be are three different people."
Unknown

Bianca

I GAPE at the box containing the cell phone on the expansive desk in front of me, wondering if this is a trick.

I'm in Rio's city office, the one above his nightclub, and the afternoon sun slants in through the floor-to-ceiling windows over near the leather settee. A pair of his goons delivered me here a few minutes ago.

One moment I was sitting outside on my suite's balcony at the estate, watching the breeze riffle through the trees down by the river as I finished my chicken salad lunch, and the next I was being ushered downstairs and into a waiting black car, to be driven here—to the club where I was first brought in all those weeks ago, trussed up like a Christmas turkey.

Weeks? I've lost track of time a little, but I think the kidnapping might have been about two months ago now.

"Is this for real? What is this, Rio?"

He grunts at my obvious shock and studies me, steepling his fingers beneath his chin. "What does it look like? I'm giving you a cell phone, Bianca."

"But I thought you didn't trust me." I'm afraid to reach out and touch it in case the phone magically disappears. I want it *so damn bad.*

"You've earned a little trust. Firstly by your behavior at the gala two weeks ago, and in the outings you've had since then."

I think back on the few visits out I've been allowed. A couple of times I asked to go to a shopping mall just because I wanted to feel normal. Not possible when you're flanked by security goons the whole way, but at least it was another connection with the outside world.

And then there's been one trip back here to the club before today, where Rio met one night with a contingent of businessmen and seemed to want me on display at the time.

I could have run on any of the mall trips—albeit with difficulty given the constant scrutiny every time I leave the estate—but there are always opportunities to slip away in a crowd. Even the best security people need to take their eyes off the prize occasionally, if only to scan their surroundings.

But I chose not to run. And I think I may have finally figured out why.

I was convinced for the longest time that I had Stockholm syndrome, but during my many hours of solitude, I've come to the realization that the need to stay has something to do with my heritage. My identity. I had a birth family—I had *parents*—who didn't abandon me as I've always thought. It wasn't for lack of love that I was handed in to that church.

Instead, they were murdered, and my nanny tried to save me from the same fate by hiding me. I need to know more. I need to find out who Bianca Carlotti really is, and the best way I can do that for now is to stay here and learn more about this strange Mafia life into which I was apparently born.

Staying has nothing to do with my complicated feelings for Rio. The whole love-hate thing that threatens to drive me crazy. No. Of course not.

I mentally roll my eyes at my own blatant self-lie.

"This is your reward for good behavior," Rio says, pushing the box toward me. "Take it."

Something as simple as a cell phone shouldn't create so much excitement and joy. I pick up the box with trembling fingers.

"Thank you." A thought strikes me. "I assume you'll monitor the usage?"

An almost smile hovers around his lips. "You assume correctly. I don't trust any person one hundred percent."

I don't know why that statement amuses me, but I find myself shaking my head and chuckling. "No. Why would you? Still, I do appreciate this."

So much more than you know. A real connection to the outside world. At last.

He nods to Danelli, standing silently by the office doorway, and I know that's my signal to leave. I clutch the box to my chest and head to the door. His office is beautiful, all dark wood, plush furniture, and expensive artwork. No wonder he enjoys doing business from here when he can.

At the door, I stop and turn back. While he's feeling

generous, I may as well ask. "Would it be all right if I call my old friend Dave? And, maybe, meet him for a quick coffee one day? Just, you know, to make sure he's recovering okay from being shot." *By your men.*

I don't say that last bit out loud, but Danelli sucks in a breath as if I've asked for something completely shocking. Perhaps I have. Perhaps in this world, people don't "do" coffee. Or platonic friendships.

Or follow up on their shooting victims.

Rio just looks at me with those darkened eyes and that inscrutable expression, and he eventually says, "Yes. That is acceptable."

Then he lowers his gaze to a set of papers in front of him on the desk, and I know I've been dismissed.

As Danelli accompanies me to the elevator where one of his men steps forward to take over chaperone duty, he touches me lightly on the arm. "I've never seen him treat anyone with the leniency with which he treats you."

I'm tempted to tease-not-tease with a response along the lines of: *What? You mean the kidnapping, the forced marriage, and the prison-like way of life since then?*

In the end, I stay silent and just nod because I know what Danelli means. Rio is proving to be a complex human being, and it's clear he does not give his trust lightly. Even if, by normal society standards, my husband is a monster, he does seem to have mellowed the tiniest bit when it comes to me. A fact that fascinates me as much as it repels.

There's a hell of a lot of responsibility on one's shoulders if a monster places his trust in you.

"Heaven help you if you ever cross the man. Keep that in mind, Bianca, for your own safety. You're beginning to grow on me, and I don't want to have to kill you."

I WAIT until I'm back at the estate and alone in my suite before calling Dave. I feel remarkably anxious about the upcoming contact, as if my old and my new life are about to collide, and I may end up as collateral damage somewhere in the middle of the two.

I don't want to have to kill you.

I certainly hope you don't, Danelli.

The conversation between Dave and me is awkward; far more stilted than I hoped or expected it to be. But then, from his point of view, he last saw me being bundled at gunpoint into the trunk of a car, and when he tried to rush forward and save me, he got shot for his efforts. Then suddenly I appear in the media, freshly married to the guy who ordered my kidnapping.

What must he have thought?

It's a wonder he takes my call at all.

"Are you really okay?" I ask for the third or fourth time, after he finally agrees to meet me at Happy Beans, a coffee shop near my old workplace.

The rescue center staff did coffee runs there all the time, and I can still recall the drink preferences of most of my work colleagues.

I like the idea of going back there to meet Dave, but at the same time, I hope I don't run into anyone else from Lots of Paws. How can I possibly explain my current situation in a way that makes sense? I can barely understand it myself.

"I've told you, Bree. I'm getting there. Much better than I was a few weeks back."

"Okay, good. That's really good." I sound so lame I want

to smack myself in the head. "And what about Shelley? She didn't, um, get…"

I can't say it out loud. It makes it all too real.

"Shot?" Dave says it for me. "No, she didn't. I was the unlucky one."

His tone is wry; slightly bitter.

"I'm so sorry," I whisper. "So sorry."

I don't know what else to say. I never knew I was secretly a Mafia baby, snatched away at birth, and planted into a so-called "normal" life. I didn't know.

"It's not your fault, Bree. Or should I call you *Bianca*?" The question must be rhetorical; he doesn't wait for a response. "And while Shelley didn't get shot, she isn't doing too well, to be honest. She quit her job a few weeks ago. Cited PTSD as the reason. Every time she turned up for work, apparently all she could think about was large men with big guns, and she kept reliving the moment she thought she'd die. As do I."

"When you go back to Lots of Paws, you mean?"

"No. I mean all the time."

Oh.

"I haven't been back, Bree. I haven't been able to bring myself to step foot back on that sidewalk, let alone walk in the door at work. I relive that moment every single night when I close my eyes."

I open my mouth to respond, but nothing comes out. Rio did that to them. My husband took away their innocence and gave them nightmares they'll probably have for the rest of their lives. My husband, whose behavior I'm kind of condoning by staying here with him and not trying to make a run for it.

Not "kind of," I correct my thoughts. *At least be honest.*

My presence *condones* his abominable behavior. And that must be horrifying for Dave and Shelley.

In the ensuing silence, Dave laughs with little humor. "Okey dokey, then. See you Friday at Happy Beans, Bree."

He rings off before I have a chance to answer.

Rio

ONLY TIME WILL TELL if I've made a grave error in trusting Bianca with her own cell phone. But the dawning excitement in her expression when she realized the phone was hers caused a frisson of something unexpected in my chest.

I will have to create more moments like that for my wife. I enjoy her smile when it becomes genuine rather than forced. It transforms her into a true beauty and reminds me of her relative innocence on our wedding night.

A sudden ache in my dick reminds me that I skipped her bed last night. I will not abstain tonight. My body craves her, like a junkie needing a fix.

A shrill ringtone interrupts the lustful train of my thoughts, the sound announcing that my caller is not an immediate member of the family. They have all been allocated a low beeping tone. This will be one of Danelli's team. But then, I already know that. I have been expecting this call for the past hour.

I punch the answer button. "Is it there?"

"Yes, Boss," comes the answer. "The shipment arrived at the docks exactly at the time they said it would. Four containers. We've checked them. It's all there."

"Good. Have Danelli contact the buyer and arrange a meet. Here at my club, Saturday night."

"Will do."

I've been distracted with thoughts of Bianca, finding myself second-guessing every decision I make and wondering what she will think. Will she judge me? Stare at me with fire and passion in her eyes, or will I only see censure?

In this case, she would have little cause for censure. A shipment of equipment to outfit a new gambling establishment is hardly the same as a consignment of drugs or weapons. It would be entirely legal, in fact, except that the trade in gambling equipment is proving a reasonable way to funnel money from some of our less salubrious arms of the company as we transition into something more aboveboard.

Most of our business these days is digitized, conducted online. Shipments like the current one are becoming rarer. Physical consignments that can be tracked mean that more things can go wrong, and make it much harder to remain under the radar of the various agencies out there who would love to bring down the Agosti family by any means they can.

Despite the mostly legal nature of this particular shipment, my gut is telling me something is off this week. I can't pinpoint exactly what it is that has raised my hackles. I have dealt with this particular buyer—from the Carbone family— several times over the years. I don't believe my unease stems from that direction.

Carlos Rossi has been lying very low of late. I have plans in train that involve him, but I have not yet given the order to go ahead on those plans, and I do not believe he is aware of what is coming.

But still, my gut says *beware*. I've only ignored my instinct once before, and my lack of action got my parents killed. I knew something was off that night, and instead of contacting my father to let him know, I brushed my concerns off as stupid and unimportant and spent the night partying at a New York hotel with three willing women.

While my father's rival gunned him down over dinner and took out my mother when she dived in front of my father to try—in vain—to save him.

I will not make that mistake again.

I need to stop thinking about sex with my wife, and get my mind back onto business matters before the wrong people die.

22

"Comforts of the past have to be left behind to achieve the dreams of the future."
Unknown

Bianca

FOUR OF RIO'S men accompany me to the Happy Beans coffee shop. At least they don't try and sit in the same booth as me, though they do a fairly obvious sweep of the place when we first arrive, and dictate where I should take a seat.

Then one pair slides into the booth behind mine, and the other pair takes up residence at a table near the door.

What would they do if I got up and sat somewhere other than where they ordered? Judging by their impassive yet alert expressions, I can guess I wouldn't like the outcome. It would probably involve being summarily bundled back into that black SUV outside and more time in isolation at Rio's estate, contemplating the error of my ways.

I sit quietly until Dave arrives, almost ten minutes after our agreed meet time. Just as I've come to the conclusion that he must have decided to stand me up, he enters the shop. He stops and stares around for a moment, as if unsure whether or not to stay. Then he spies me and starts forward.

He is using a cane, and his limping progress across the café is slow. Despite the fact that he's tall and decently built, he seems smaller than I remember. Less virile. My heart aches for what might have been between us.

What likely *would* have been, until Rio tore our lives to pieces.

That budding interest I felt on my birthday—the hope that Dave would finally ask me out and we could explore the thread of attraction between us—is gone. Drowned in the wake of the tsunami that Rio unleashed upon my life, my body...and my heart.

Finally, Dave reaches my booth and stands there, staring down at me. Is he wondering whether or not he should hug me? I jump to my feet, intending to take the initiative, but he flinches back, and I freeze at the unexpected slight.

He slides into the booth, angling his injured leg so it juts out a little. And I'm left standing there feeling foolish for expecting a hug under the circumstances. Why on earth would he hug me? He probably hates me for what he thinks is a betrayal of our friendship.

I *married* the man who ordered him shot. And yes, I was forced into marrying Rio, but with at least a couple of chances to run since then, I have to accept responsibility for the fact that I've chosen to stay.

Slowly, I slide back onto my own seat, my cheeks warm. "Sorry, I just thought…"

I don't know what my jumbled brain planned to say. My thoughts are whirling at the sight of him. My real life suddenly feels like a distant memory, and I don't quite know how to reconnect with the part of myself that was Bree—or how to reconnect with Dave, for that matter.

His gaze is reproachful as he settles in and stares at me. "You came here with the same big men and their guns that populate my nightmares," he says, and I glance around at the goons, horror leaching through me.

"Oh my God. Was it one of these guys?" That whole experience was a blur of terror. I don't think Rio would assign any of the men from that night to watch over me now. Would he?

As I meet the gaze of one of the goons who took the next booth along, the guy—I think his name is Leon—surreptitiously shakes his head.

Okay. Not one of these guys, then. Relief slackens my muscles, and I lean back against the bench seat. Then sit up as the realization strikes. Oh. So they really are listening in.

While I'm processing that, Dave lets out a snort. "I am trying not to look at them at all, Bree. I didn't mean literally. I meant the comment metaphorically. Are they here to protect Gregorio Agosti's new marital asset? His *wife*?"

He almost spits when he says Rio's name. I frown at the vitriol, trying to steer the conversation into something less controversial than guns and my husband.

"I already ordered our coffees," I say. "Same as what we always had in the past. I hope that's okay?"

Doubt assails me. I should have waited. For all I know, he

now hates lattes with a light dusting of chocolate on top and only drinks tea.

"That's fine, Bree. Thanks. It is good to see you, actually."

Really? Could have fooled me.

At my raised eyebrows, he laughs. The dry sound seems to release a little of the tension that has held us both since he walked in.

He leans forward, adjusting his position and laying his hands on the table, and on impulse, I reach over and grab his fingers. He jerks beneath my grip, then settles, allowing the touch.

"I thought you were going to turn up dead after that night," he admits. "Did you know they were coming for you?"

I release his hands and tuck mine down tightly into my lap. All the better to hide the tremble. "Of course I didn't know! I've never had anything to do with...well, you know..."

"Mafia? Huh. Me either. Until that night."

"Are you really okay, Dave? Are you healing?"

He nods. "Yeah. The docs said I'll probably have a permanent limp, but I won't always need this." He taps the head of the cane, resting against the side of the bench seat. "It'll just take time, and a ton of physical therapy, to get back strength and muscle tone."

"That's good. I mean, not about the limp, but about the fact that it will mostly heal."

The server arrives at that moment to deposit our coffees on the table and, when we decline food, wanders off to take an order from another table.

177

"I read about your past in the media," he says, not touching his drink. "It's all over the internet. The fact that you were a Carlotti once upon a time. A Mafia princess. I did some research while I was convalescing. That family—*your* family, I guess— was apparently once as powerful as the Agostis are today."

"Yes, so I've been told. The media have been enjoying the fact that I emerged seemingly out of nowhere."

"And you can't deny they're fascinated by the fact that you married the bastard who kidnapped you off the street. You fucking *married* him, Bree? Come on. Why the *fuck* would you do that?"

Pain darkens his expression, and I wrap my arms around my middle, trying to hold in the sob that wants to burst free.

That's the million-fucking-dollar question.

I decide to be as honest as I can with him. He deserves no less from me. After all, he did try to save my life that day, and he's entitled to his bitterness now.

"At first, I think I was in shock." My voice is husky, and I clear my throat before continuing. "I was numb. Then utterly terrified. Then I became angry. So damn angry. I did try to escape once. But Rio did what he does best. He threatened to hurt the people I care about if I didn't do as he commanded. You, and Shelley, and everyone else who works at Lots of Paws. Probably my dad too, if he can ever find him in the remote Thailand mountains.

"Then, through the discovery that I'd been born Bianca Carlotti, I realized I hadn't been abandoned by my birth parents as I'd always thought. I want to know more about who I was—who I *am*. And learn as much about my birth family as I can. There are people in Rio's circle who knew them, Dave. Stefano and Rina Carlotti. They were real, and from what I've heard so far, they truly loved me. They handed me over to the nanny to hide me because they suspected what was coming and wanted to protect me."

I blink hard, determined not to cry. Besides, I need to gather my courage for the next bit, which is much harder to admit to anyone other than myself.

I take a deep breath and let it out slowly. "Later, I found there was something about Rio...something that drew me in and held me...something I've never felt before..."

"What? *Love*?" His tone is dismissive until he looks deep into my eyes and reads the truth buried there.

"*Jesus*, Bree! You actually *love* him? You fucking love *Rio Agosti*?" His lip curls up, transforming his face into a look that can only be described as disgusted.

I sit up straighter in my seat. "Please don't call me Bree, Dave. If you've been reading up on me, then you know I go by the name Bianca now."

His mouth thins. "Wow. I have no words. I mean, *wow*." He lifts a hand and runs it through his hair, leaving the blond mop more ruffled than it usually is. "You've changed, Bree. I mean, *Bianca*. I never expected that of you. He's a *murderer*, for Christ's sake. A common criminal. A—"

"Rio Agosti is many things, but he is not *common*. And as awful as this whole situation has been the past couple of months, he is also now my husband."

Dave gapes at me as if he has no idea who I am anymore, and then he shakes his head. "He's really done a number on you, hasn't he? Jesus, the Bree I knew would never have let herself fall under the spell of a Mafia murderer. *Never*."

I slide out of the booth and stand, leaving my coffee untouched. This meeting was clearly a huge mistake. I should have left it at the phone call. "The thing is, Dave, I'm not Bree. Not anymore. And I guess you never knew the real me.

Which isn't surprising, given *I* never knew the real me either. I just didn't realize that until I met Rio."

I nod to Leon, the security guy who answered my unspoken query earlier, indicating that I'm ready to leave. "I'm so sorry you got hurt, Dave. It is truly terrible what happened to you. And I'm sorry that Shelley is experiencing PTSD. I suspect I'll have that too, at some point, when all is said and done and I stop tamping everything down.

"But I need to find out more about who I am, and…and… Yes, I do hate who he is and a lot of what he does, but I *have* fallen for Rio. I never wanted or expected to, but that's how it is. And I need to understand what that means for me moving forward."

I lift my chin and walk away from Dave and his still-horrified expression. Away from my old life. Away from everything safe and familiar. Away from all the hopes and dreams about my future and the beautiful things I used to think my future may hold.

And I can barely see the exit for my tears.

23

"... there are no wrong turns, only unexpected paths."
Mark Nepo

Bianca

I SPEND the next twenty-four hours holed up in my suite,
crying quietly into the pillows for the loss of my innocence.
That's how I see her—*Bree*. She was my innocent side.
Before Rio.

I don't think she's there inside me anymore, but I still
don't know who and what Bianca is. I refuse dinner, much to
Francine's disgust, and lie curled in the fetal position in the
middle of my huge bed for most of the night, wondering if
Rio will visit me.

Praying he won't, because I don't have the emotional
strength to deal with his all-encompassing presence
right now.

Devastated when he doesn't. Because every atom of my body craves him, every waking moment. Where is he? Why has he not come to my bed the way he has most nights in recent weeks? Has he found someone else, now that he doesn't need me to sign over my family's business?

God, I'm a mess. I'm a goddamn fucking emotional wreck.

Sometime near dawn, I finally drop off to sleep, only to wake with a jerk a few hours later as a sudden realization strikes.

I sit bolt upright, clutching at my belly. I am three weeks overdue for my cycle.

Blood drains from my cheeks, and I feel as if I'm about to pass out. I stagger to the bathroom and splash cool water onto my face before staring at my reflection in the huge, gilt-edged mirror above the sink.

Shocked eyes stare back at me. I may be carrying Rio's child.

Francine chooses that inopportune moment to knock and enter my suite. I hear her bustling around in the lounge area, opening the balcony doors to let in the morning breeze as she does every day if the weather is nice. She hums a little, the clink of crockery and cutlery indicating she's setting up my breakfast at the table near the window.

She sounds happier than usual. I wonder what has prompted that. It can't be anything related to me. I curve my hand protectively around my stomach. She doesn't know that life as we all know it may be about to change forever.

I take an extra minute or two to dry my face before heading out to greet her. She will no doubt force me to eat, given I skipped dinner last night, and the knowledge sends a fresh wave of nausea through my system.

No wonder I've had bouts of feeling unwell lately, if I truly am pregnant. I had put my lack of hunger down to anxiety, but now…

I can't process the idea that I may actually be carrying Rio's child. It will change everything if I am.

I'm going to have to get a test done, somehow, without anyone else finding out.

I take a couple of deep breaths, and when I feel steady, I head out to the lounge.

"Morning, Francine." I'm proud of how calm I sound, when inside I'm quaking with so many churning emotions. "You sound chirpy today."

"Good morning. I *am* feeling…chirpy, as you put it. Tommaso is arriving today for a longer visit. As you know, he only stayed briefly last time to attend Rio's wedding."

And mine. I bite back a grin. She is so very focused on her family, but clearly, I haven't yet been accepted in her mind as part of that elite clique.

"That's exciting for you, Francine."

I take a seat at the breakfast table, pleased to see toast as part of the offering this morning. I can manage toast. I think.

"It is." She shoots me a big genuine-looking smile, and the sight is so unexpected on her usually dour face I almost laugh. "He manages the Philadelphia arm of the business for Rio, and I don't see him as often as I'd like."

Her smile disappears as quickly as it came. "You will have to eat today, my dear. Rio stayed in the city last night, preparing for something this evening. He has requested you attend him at his club later, so you will need proper sustenance today."

"Do you know what it is he has planned? What he wants me there for?"

Francine's expression doesn't change. "I don't ask the details, dear. But it will be late, I believe. And you will need to dress up. I will be back later to help you, if you need it."

A surge of gratitude passes through me, and with it, sadness for the woman before me. The question blurts out of me without thought. "Don't you ever want *more* than simply being Rio's housekeeper, Francine? Do you have your own home, and interests, and…well, life? Could you not move to Philly to be closer to Tommaso?"

I trail off at the shocked look in her eyes.

"This *is* my home. Rio, his brothers, and sister—I love them all as much as I do my own son. I would do anything for any of them. This is my world, Bianca, and I'm happy in a role where I can be of service."

She turns to leave, clearly upset.

"I'm sorry," I call out as she reaches the door. "I didn't mean to upset you. I just…well, really, I wanted to say thank you for looking after me so well."

Something softens in her expression. "You are welcome, my dear. I can tell Rio is very taken with you, and that is important to everyone here. I believe, in time, you and he will find true happiness together."

Happiness? With Rio? My hand inadvertently goes to my stomach, and I rest my fingers across the area where a baby may be growing. I need to know, one way or the other.

"Would you mind asking the security team on duty if they would take me shopping today?"

Her eyes immediately narrow as if she suspects a trick.

"I was feeling a little down last night, but I'm sure some retail therapy will help lighten my mood. I'll be back with plenty of time to prepare to visit Rio at the club. Please?"

After a moment, she nods. "Very well." She looks pointedly at the food remaining on the table. "As long as you eat."

In answer, I pick up my buttered toast and munch into it determinedly, shooting her a quick grin around the mouthful.

She shakes her head and huffs out a chuckle. "Be ready in an hour, then, Bianca. I will let them know you need...*retail therapy*."

She wrinkles her nose at the term before turning to leave, and I force myself to eat the toast and then a small bowl of fresh fruit salad, too.

I'm still not sure, of course, but if it *is* possible I'm carrying Rio's child, I need to start looking after myself. And that means no more skipping meals.

IN THE END, it isn't as difficult as I expect to quietly get hold of a pregnancy test kit. Once Rio began letting me out, he provided some cash to use for things such as coffees or incidentals. Pin money, he called it in a slightly old-fashioned way, though the amount is far too excessive to be considered "pin money" in my view—unless I get into the habit of buying coffee made with liquid gold.

I explain to the goons on duty today that I need to stop in at a pharmacy for "women's stuff," and while they do accompany me into the store, they at least give me some privacy when I head determinedly for the female products section.

I pay with cash and tuck my purchase discreetly away in my oversized purse where it burns a hole while I pretend to enjoy the rest of the shopping trip. I end up buying an unnecessary set of lingerie just so I can show that the trip was not without purpose, if anyone happens to ask.

When I'm back at the estate, I hide the kit in a bundle of clothing in my huge walk-in dressing room. I can't bring myself to do the test just yet. Though it's the only thing I can think about all afternoon and into the evening.

Francine dutifully arrives after dinner to help me dress, approving my choice of a skintight red dress that has a low neckline and skims my legs above the knee, giving it a slightly party-like feel. I pair it with spiky heels and pin back some of my hair with yet another diamond-encrusted silver clip that matches my dangly earrings, leaving the bulk of my hair to tumble down my back.

I'm becoming less awkward in heels and makeup now. It almost feels good to "paint" on my face as it helps hide my emotions and provides a buffer—if only a mental one—between me and all the sets of eyes that study my every move.

"Good choice," Francine says as she zips up my dress and then pats me gently on the shoulder to indicate she's done. "The red highlights your coloring. It complements your skin tone and dark hair beautifully, Bianca. You are a very attractive young lady."

"Thank you." I study my reflection in the full-length mirror in the dressing area, feeling more "Bianca" and less "Bree" by the moment.

My gaze drops to my stomach—it is as flat as it's always been.

Maybe I'm wrong. Maybe I'm just late. Or maybe the nervous tension of the past couple of months has simply thrown my body's hormones into chaos.

The thought that I may not be pregnant after all is strangely disconcerting. I can't figure out if I'm hoping for a positive or negative outcome. Either way, my nerves are stretched so tight that energy buzzes through me, making it difficult to remain still.

"Will you give me a few minutes, please, Francine? I just want to touch up my makeup and hair. Tell the boys I'll be ready to leave in fifteen minutes."

Rio's aunt nods and leaves to pass on the message. I scurry over to where I hid the test kit earlier and pull it out. There's no way I can get through tonight without knowing for sure one way or the other.

Time to find out the truth.

THERE MUST BE something universal about the stress of peeing on a pregnancy stick and awaiting the result. Whether or not a woman wants it to be positive or negative, the waiting feels like torture.

This moment in time could change my life irrevocably. Or it could simply be a false alarm. I pace the bathroom, back and forth, my heels clicking on the marble and sweat coating my palms as I wring my hands together.

If it *is* positive, will Rio be happy? Or angry? How will *I* feel?

My breath shortens and my heart pounds as I finally stop pacing and stare down at the stick now showing a very clear result.

Two lines. Not faint at all. A very decisive positive.

I am pregnant with the child of a Mafia crime boss.

24

"Avoiding danger is no safer in the long run than outright exposure. Life is either a daring adventure, or nothing."
Helen Keller

Rio

I NEED Bianca by my side this evening because I missed being with her last night. I don't want to admit that to anyone, but if there is one thing I am—with myself at least—it's honest.

It took everything in me to allow her to attend that coffee date with her friend. He knew her, before. He tried to save her life. If she saw that as heroic… If she realized what she was missing and decided she wanted to go back to that way of life, I would have to step in and stop her from doing so.

And her hatred for me would likely rise all over again.

The report I had from the team on duty that day was pleasing. They said she defended me to her old friend. And she admitted to him that she loves me.

Thoughts of Bianca fill my head when I should be focusing on business. But I've come to enjoy her slightly besotted expression when she looks at me now. I listen for the increased tempo in her breathing when I enter the room, and I enjoy the slight pink that colors her cheeks even while she pretends to everyone around us that I have no effect on her at all.

I know the truth about what my presence does for her.

And what hers does for me. Everything about Bianca Carlotti-Agosti turns me on.

I imagine sinking into her willing body, or sliding my hard cock between her hot, eager lips and allowing her beautiful mouth to suck me dry. My dick twitches into instant semihardness.

I want her. More than I've ever wanted any woman. And yet, I know that wanting her makes me weak. I cannot afford weakness in a world in which the slightest hint of vulnerability could mean a lessening of my power and control.

It could mean chaos. Or death.

My need for Bianca makes me vulnerable, but I can't seem to switch it off.

Despite that, having her beside me at the club tonight feels right. She has shown that she can be trusted, to an extent at least, and I like the idea of drawing her further into our family business, albeit in the smallest of ways to start with.

The meet with the buyer's representatives should be straightforward. The Carbone family is already aware of the product and price. They have received similar shipments from us several times before. Our negotiations have already been completed. This will be merely a courtesy meet to conclude the contract, and I will take the opportunity to tell them that this will be the last shipment of its kind.

My senses are telling me to be cautious, but I don't believe the possible danger stems from the Carbone deal.

I push the intercom button on my desk and ask my PA, Dana, to call Danelli into my office.

"Be extra alert tonight," I say when he puts his head around the door. "Just in case. Extra teams on duty, and I need everyone carrying."

Danelli straightens and comes all the way into the room, carefully closing the door behind him. "Really, Boss? Should we postpone the meet, then? Your instincts are usually spot-on. I can—"

"No," I cut across him. "I want this done and the shipment collected by tomorrow night at the latest. I simply need you to be ready for anything. Not just tonight but all the time. Rossi has been very quiet of late."

"Yes, Boss."

He turns to leave, worry dipping his brows together. Good. I want him concerned. *I'm* concerned, and I do not like that state of being at all.

As he reaches the door, he looks back at me. "And Bianca? Do you want her back at the estate? She's on her way here already, but I can always tell them to turn around and take her home."

For a few seconds, I debate back and forth in my head. I don't know what has me so jittery, but my gut says I'm making the right decision bringing her into the city tonight. "My wife stays with me through this. But make sure there's extra protection at the estate tonight, too."

Danelli's frown deepens. "Yes, sir."

He heads off to, presumably, arrange additional security and ensure everyone is armed and ready for anything.

Perhaps after tonight, I will be able to put aside this niggling doubt that something isn't as it seems. Until then, Bianca will remain by my side where I can better protect her, if it becomes necessary.

And if all goes smoothly at the meet, I will be in a position to bed her more quickly.

Tonight, I intend to take my wife up to my rooms above the club and fuck her until she screams for mercy. For oblivion. But not before we both ascend to heaven when she wraps her arms and legs around me, and I release my hot and willing seed deep inside her beautifully tight pussy.

Bianca is mine, and tonight I intend to stake my claim in a way that ensures she forgets everything about her past, and knows that *I* am her only option for the future.

Bianca

I EXPECT to ascend the elevator to Rio's penthouse apartment, or at least to the level where his office is situated, but instead, the goons take me straight to the VIP area of the club. It is late, already after eleven, but I guess in this world of darkness, meetings at night are commonplace, and 11:00 p.m. in clubland is probably considered early, not late.

The music hums through me in a low *thump thump thump* as I spy Rio in the mezzanine lounge area above the dance floor. He is sitting on one of the couches in a relaxed pose, his arms outstretched along the back of the couch and one ankle resting lightly on his other knee.

He looks brooding and sexy, and I wish I had the courage to simply sashay right up to him and climb confidently onto his lap, mushing my pussy against his groin and ignoring everyone else in the area.

I don't do anything of the sort, of course. Instead, I simply walk toward him, past the VIP bar where I sat to watch his business dealings last time I was here. As I near him, a female server arrives ahead of me and bends forward to deliver him a tray of drinks. The move thrusts her ample breasts right into his face, and jealousy rears up inside me, fast and unexpected.

He's mine.

The sensation of the music in my veins is almost tribal, primitive. The beat seems to suit my wild mood.

Mine. Mine. Mine.

Part of me is terrified to tell him my news, and the other part wants to blurt it out and gauge his reaction.

He is my husband. And soon, he will be the father of my child.

How will he feel about that?

He ignores the server, and she pouts and moves away. His gaze remains fixed on me, intense and unreadable, and I can't help the slightly exaggerated sway of my hips as I make my way across the last of the space to close the gap between us.

It doesn't seem to matter what my brain thinks. My body automatically switches into sexy mode whenever Rio is nearby.

I stop in front of him and stare down, waiting to hear what he wants from me. I am both desperate to speak, and equally desperate to keep my secret for just a little while longer.

The push-pull is no different from anything else I've felt when it comes to interactions with this man. He inspires conflict within me at every turn.

As if he senses my inner turmoil, his eyes narrow slightly. Then his mouth curves up at the corners. Does he enjoy the knowledge that he has me going around in circles with my emotions?

He pats the seat next to him and, when I comply, lowers his hand to stroke my thigh. The flesh is exposed as my dress has ridden up slightly, and the feel of his fingertips against my skin causes goose bumps to rise up in the wake of his touch.

I lift my chin and meet his gaze. In that moment, he allows his mask to slip. The burning passion I read in the depths of his eyes causes my breath to catch in my throat.

"You look beautiful, Bianca. Sexy as fuck." His voice is low and raspy, and yet I can hear him perfectly despite the thrum of music in the background.

It is as if my system is finely tuned to him, and even with the sounds of a club full of people rising around us and trying to invade our space, somehow there is only Rio.

"But then, you always do," he adds.

"You didn't come to me last night." *Shit*. I don't mean to say that, but the accusation just pops straight out of my mouth.

One of his brows rises briefly. "Did you miss me, wife?"

Now it's my turn to narrow my eyes. "What do you think?"

"Say it."

"Why?"

"*Say it.*"

The command hints at something desperate. Something

that feeds my desire. Rio is not as in control as he wants everyone to believe.

I smile at him and lean close. I love the sound of his breath sucking in that way. I love the delicious scent of him that rises up and assails my nostrils. Need pools between my legs.

Can he smell it? My desire? I hope so. I am wet and yearning for his touch. I want the sensation of his fingers right there against my clit. Stroking along and around my seam. Sliding up into my channel in a promise of more to come.

"Yes, I missed you, Rio. A lot. And I don't want to sleep alone tonight. *Husband.*"

His hand comes up and circles my throat. He squeezes, lightly, as if reminding me—or perhaps himself—who is in charge. I know exactly who's in charge in this moment. He could do anything to me, and I would let him.

"Rio, I want you so—"

"Boss, they're here."

Danelli's voice and his looming presence break the spell, and Rio releases me and leans back with a tiny groan. I doubt anyone else can hear that sound over the music, but I'm close enough to catch the regret.

"Soon, Bianca. I promise you."

"Good."

Then the emotionless mask is back in place, and he turns his attention to a group of suited businessmen walking toward our cluster of couches. Rio rises and draws me to my feet before cementing me to his side with a firm grip.

I flinch a little as I rub up against the metal beneath his arm. Rio is carrying a gun.

I flick a glance around and realize there are more of his security here than usual. Far more. They are everywhere. What is going on? Is it dangerous to be here tonight? Should I leave? It's not just me to think about now; it's my baby… *Our* baby…

As my thoughts fly around and my heart rate increases, I realize Rio would not deliberately put me in danger. Even without his knowledge of our child, he cares more for me than he wanted or planned to. I'm not sure how I know that, but I do. He cares for me a great deal, in his own twisted way.

"Carbone." Rio's tone is tight. "Take a seat. We have business to discuss."

The shorter man in the center of the cluster of security turns his gaze on me. I suppress an instant shiver at the coldness in his features. He looks a little like Carlos Rossi, but without the grandfatherly twinkle.

"With *her* here?"

"You mean my wife, Bianca Carlotti-Agosti? You will address Bianca with respect. Or lose your tongue."

At my mewl of distress, Rio's arm tightens, holding me firmly in place when I try to shift away.

After a moment, the other man nods respectfully in my direction. "My mistake, Mrs. Agosti. It is a pleasure to meet you."

I can't do anything but nod. If I speak, I may accidentally let fly with a moan, or start crying. Would Rio really cut out the man's tongue? I slip my arm around Rio's waist. If I don't, I'm afraid my shaking legs may not hold me up.

We are all in the process of taking our seats once again on the various couches when screaming breaks out below, and the music screeches to a sudden halt.

I don't even have time to glance down there to see what's going on. There is the weird sound of a *pop, pop, pop*, then a series of loud blasts, and then Rio throws himself on top of me, crashing us down to the floor as all hell breaks loose around us.

25

"Reality sucks, I want my dreams back."
Sandra Chami Kassis

Bianca

THE CARPETED floor is sticky against my cheek. It smells disgusting, like stale liquor.

I will have to tell Rio that he needs a new cleaning crew when this is over. Stupid inane thoughts keep popping into my head, as if time has stopped and I actually have the ability to consider them in a bubble of calm amidst the chaos.

Am I dead? Is this what it feels like to be dead?

Yes, he definitely needs a new cleaning crew.

The screams intensify; the gunshots are louder.

Chaos intruding on the calm.

I realize my mouth is open, and I'm contributing to the

sound of the screams. But I can't seem to shut off the panicked noise erupting up out of my throat.

I clutch at Rio's shirt, feeling his heart pounding against my chest and hearing his growl of rage as he reaches for his gun.

No! I scrabble at his arm. No more guns. *No more*.

But he evades my grip and rolls off me, up onto his knees. He points his gun and shoots before I can stop him. The blast is so loud it deafens me. I want to yell at him to stay down. To stay safe. To let his men do what is needed and keep him from getting a bullet. He's the target; he has to be.

Who else would they be gunning for? Whoever *they* are.

He's going to be a father, and he may be dead in a few seconds. *I* may be dead in a few seconds' time.

And my baby…

I curl up my legs until I'm lying in a tight little ball, my arms around my knees. I think I may be rocking back and forth. I can't tell. There is too much movement and noise and the screaming and gunfire… It's everywhere around me.

I should close my eyes. I don't want to see death coming for me and my baby.

But I can't seem to stop looking. And death has taken up residence in every direction.

The businessman with the cold eyes is lying on the floor a few feet away from me. At least, he *had* cold eyes. Now, he just looks vacant; empty.

Even as I gape at him, noting the blood-rimmed hole in his throat, I hear a voice calling my name.

"Bianca. Move. Now." It's Leon the goon, crawling toward me across the floor. He grips my arm and drags me to my feet. "Move, woman."

I just keep staring at him. I can't seem to make my brain

work. Or my limbs. He shoves me forward, not in the direction of the elevator but the other way, down a hallway and toward a set of stairs I never even knew existed.

He shields me with his body as he drags me away from the fight.

"Wait!" Jesus Christ, am I still screaming? Finally, I manage to control the sound, swallowing down the terror until only the occasional moan escapes. "Rio. Where is he? Is he—"

"Danelli has him covered. I need to get you to saf—"

Pop pop pop. Leon's eyes widen as he stares at me, then his mouth slackens, and the life simply disappears out of his features. He crumples to the floor at my feet.

I stare down at him. He's dead, too? Just like that. I've been there when animals have had to be euthanized at the rescue center, but I've never seen a human being die. Right in front of my eyes. One moment alive and the next...*nothing*.

I look back and see men still firing guns, yelling, screaming, people running all over the place, around the dead bodies, slipping in all the blood...

Where is my husband?

I stumble back toward the bar. I don't even know what I'm planning. Where I'm going. What I'm supposed to do in this mess of horror.

Then I realize I'm screeching his name. "*Rio. Rio.*" Over and over. *There.* I see him, gun raised and pointing at someone. Who? Is that... "*Anders*?"

Carlos Rossi's man. Why is he here? Why is he pointing a gun at Rio? Why is...

Oh, okay, Anders is dead too. My husband just shot him. Right in the face. He has no face left. I gape down at the mess of blood and bone and brain matter all over the floor. He *was* Anders. He's not anymore.

Nothing is making sense to me. I want this to be over. I want to go home. I want my old life. I want…

I fall to my knees and begin to sob.

I want Rio.

Rio

I BROUGHT BIANCA INTO A BLOODBATH. I can't even turn my head to see if my men got her to safety. Because if I do, I'm dead. And if I'm dead, she'll follow me into oblivion as soon as Rossi's men get to her.

Rage burns through my blood, but I will not give in to its distracting effect.

Stay focused. Survive. And then payback will follow as surely as the sun will rise in the morning.

The danger I sensed wasn't from the Carbone deal. At least I was correct about that. It was Carlos Rossi, waiting in the wings. I will cut him into *fucking pieces* when I catch up with the man who threatened my world. My family. My wife.

I was banking on his fondness for Rina Carlotti to stay his hand, at least in relation to Bianca. She looks like her mother, and Rossi was besotted with the woman when they were younger. I misjudged, and now my family may be about to pay the consequences. Just like before, when my inattention led to my parents' deaths.

Danelli and two of his men are trying to hustle me out of the area, but I refuse to budge. This is my miscalculation to fix.

Rossi's second raises his weapon, deathly intent in his gaze. I fire first, straight into Anders's face. No chance to miss at this range. The body drops, and just like that, the fight is over.

Only it isn't over, not by a long shot, because Danelli pulls me aside, and his words fill me with dread. "The estate was hit too. Not sure how many are down, or who. It's chaos out there, apparently."

"Find out. *Now*. My brother. My aunt. My cousin. They are all staying at the estate tonight."

As would Bianca have been, if I had not had the instinct to bring her here.

"Yes, sir." His expression is impassive, but his eyes are worried. "As soon as I know, you'll know."

He directs his men to round up the remainder of Rossi's crew, herding them into a group and forcing them all to their knees in front of the bar. Then he steps off to the side, talking into his earpiece.

Carbone is dead, caught in the middle of a feud neither of us saw coming. Two of his men are down too, the remaining men he brought with him already on their phones, talking urgently to whoever does their cleanup.

I am unlikely to be their target for revenge. They know Anders too—everyone in the city does—and they know that means it must be Rossi at the heart of this attempted hit.

I stride over to the cowering bastards from Rossi's crew, all of whom stare up at me with fear in their eyes. *Good.* I raise my gun and point it at each of them, one after the other. The terror in their expressions feeds my inner sadistic beast. He has been dormant for some time. Pacified by the presence of Bianca.

I took my eyes off the business. And look where that got us. No more.

When I transfer my gaze to the final guy, his mouth is opening and closing as he convulsively swallows, and sweat coats his brow. I grin at him, and he flinches backward.

What does he see in my eyes? His death? My inner beast?

I place my gun at the top of his nose between his eyes and lean down close. "You are today's lucky one. You get to live and deliver a message to your boss."

The man lets out a strange groan, but he gives a quick nod.

"Tell Rossi I'm coming for him. I'm coming for his family. His children. His fucking *grandchildren*. His world. I'm going to destroy everything he holds dear. And I'm going to save him for last so he can watch his empire crumble and fall. Got that?"

The man nods again and whimpers, and I grab his arm and lift him roughly to his feet.

"Go, then. Back to your boss. And I will know if you don't deliver my message word for word. Trust me. *I will know*."

As the man scurries off, the sound of feminine sobbing enters my consciousness. I look up then to see Bianca on her knees, one arm wrapped tightly across her middle and the other fisted against her mouth.

Her eyes, staring straight at me, are haunted.

Filled with nothing but horror and revulsion.

"You can love a monster, it can even love you back, but that doesn't change its nature."
Eliza Crewe, *Crushed*

Bianca

I KEEP my fist shoved against my mouth because if I don't, more screams may burst out and this time never stop. I'm about to shatter and break into a million tiny pieces. I'm pretty sure the father of my baby is about to execute those men huddled on their knees in front of him.

If he does, that will make his head count for today six, if you include the one from earlier. Anders.

Do I count Anders? He was about to shoot Rio and no doubt me directly after that, so that one at least could be deemed self-defense. Protecting his own. Protecting me.

But the others…

Are they about to die, simply because they're on the wrong side in a war that never seems to end? *Is* this a war? Is that the right term?

I stare around the room, at the bodies and the blood. At the men on their knees in front of Rio, staring up at their probable executioner with the knowledge of impending death in their eyes.

Yes. This *is* a war. A war for the city of Boston and beyond. A war with power and money and control as the ultimate prize.

And my husband is at the center of it all.

My brain stops working at this point. I can't process anything more about this situation. It's too horrific.

Someone drags me up to my feet. Pulls me into a firm chest. Holds me tight. Rocks me. Whoever it is smells good. *Safe*. His scent masks the smell of blood and death, at least for a few seconds. I sink into the embrace, grateful for the reprieve.

Who knew death could smell so overwhelmingly awful?

I realize my name is being called, over and over.

"Bianca. *Bianca*! *La mia bella moglie*. Little bird. Come back to me. Ah, there you are. Back with us again."

I blink up at Rio. He's the one holding me. The one who has given me a sense of safety. The one calling me back from wherever I went. He still has a gun clutched in his hand.

A crazed laugh lurches out of me at the irony. "We made it through a hailstorm of bullets, Rio. You, me, and the baby."

The announcement tumbles unexpectedly from my mouth, which doesn't seem connected to my brain right now.

I didn't mean to tell him this way. I wasn't sure I would tell him at all.

I'm still laughing. Why can't I stop?

His brows rise and his mouth drops open. So that's what a jaw-dropping moment looks like. Then he snaps it shut. There's a sudden tic in his cheek, a raw look in his expression that I've never seen before. For the first time since I laid eyes on Rio after my kidnapping, he seems...uncertain.

"You can't be... Are you..." His brows become the only expressive part of his face. They lower, pulling together in a frown. "You must be in shock, Bianca." He turns and barks an order to someone. "Get her out of here. Now."

"Yes, Boss. Where—"

"Not the estate. Obviously. Take her to my boat. It's moored at the Constitution Marina."

The estate. Danelli's earlier words flitter to the top of my mind. *The estate was hit too.*

"Francine? Is she okay? I hope she's okay." I don't even particularly like the woman. But she's been growing on me lately. The ferocity with which she loves and serves her family—*my* family now—is deserving of respect. "Her son was arriving today. She was so happy."

Rio gives me a tiny shake and leans forward to stare intently into my face. He's truly rattled. Can the others see it? I suspect not. But I'm beginning to know him. And I glimpse his fear deep behind those dark eyes. I think he *lets* me see it, just for a moment, though I'm not sure why he would allow anyone—even me—to see his vulnerability.

Somehow, I sense he's not afraid for himself. Instead, Rio is afraid for his family. He's afraid for me. And he's deathly afraid for our baby.

At least we have that in common.

I almost reach up a hand to cup his cheek, comfort him... until I remember all the bodies. And the blood. I clench my fingers into a fist instead and keep my hand by my side.

"Bianca," he says in a low tone. "Go now with Matteo. Do what he says, when he says it. I will join you when..." He flicks a glance around and then returns to me. "When I can."

"Are you going to kill them all now?"

His eyes soften for a second. "Do not think about it, little bird. I want you safe. You and..."

His gaze drops to my belly, the contemplation like a gentle caress.

I spread the fingers of one hand wide over my still-flat stomach, like I can protect the little one from the violent scene in which its parents stand. I open my mouth to say something, but I'm not even sure what I intend. I don't seem to be thinking very clearly right now.

Before I can articulate my chaotic thoughts, a goon I've not met before steps forward and grips my upper arm. He's not rough, though. More insistent than anything.

"Come, Mrs. Agosti."

This must be Matteo. I guess. I allow myself to be dragged away from Rio and the horrific scene that I will likely see in my nightmares from now until the day I die. But when we reach the door, I can't help turning back to look.

Like a bystander at a car crash. I don't want to look. I don't want to see. But I simply can't help myself.

Rio stands in the middle of the carnage, still staring at me. He looks like the devil himself, tall, dark, and brooding amidst the fallen in his bloody kingdom of Hell.

Is it worth it, Rio? The price you all pay for power in this terrible world?

I turn to Matteo. "What does *la mia bella moglie* mean?"

A huff of breath from the man beside me, then he says quietly, "It means, my beautiful wife."

I start to turn and follow, then notice the female server

from earlier, crawling out from behind the bar on her hands and knees. Back when I last saw her—before the attack—she annoyed the hell out of me with her obvious fawning over Rio. Now, I'm glad to see she made it, as did some of the other serving staff.

Not all did. There are nightclub staff among the bodies on the floor. What did Rio call Dave and Shelley once? Collateral damage. Incidentals.

Is everyone around Rio an incidental?

Perhaps the bar is reinforced, just in case of this very situation. If I were in Rio's shoes, I'd reinforce everything around me. All the time.

Matteo tugs at my arm, dispelling the random thoughts, and shoves me through the door into the almost-hidden hallway.

As I do so, I cringe at the sudden sound of the now-familiar *pop-pop-pop*. Is that Rio pulling the trigger, or is it one of his men? Does it matter who? They are all murderers.

But only one of them is the father of your child.

I scurry away like a coward, following Matteo and knowing there is nothing I can do to save those men. As he guides me downstairs and into a waiting dark car, I wonder if this violent world is the only possible destiny for my child.

Rio

IF I COULD CHANGE anything from today, it would be to ensure that Bianca was nowhere near this bloodbath. The devastation in her eyes when she stared at me...and then that one little comment... It destroyed me. *She* destroyed me.

She's carrying my child.

I've never been more stunned in my life. And in this moment more than any other, I cannot afford to be distracted.

My cheeks paled when she made the announcement. I could feel the blood leach away from my face. Could she sense my shock? I could tell from her expression she didn't even know what she was saying. Was it the truth, or was her mind wandering because of what she'd just witnessed?

I believe she was telling the truth. I feel it in my bones. I am going to become a father.

I rub my hand over my face as if I can scrub away the dirtiness of this life. But of course I cannot. I need to focus. I need to figure out how to manage this fucking debacle. I need to find out if my brother is still alive. My aunt. My cousin.

Fuck.

Rossi will pay for this.

The sound of shots rings out behind me, and I whirl, instinctively raising my gun. But I don't need to use it. The five men who worked for Rossi are no more. One of Danelli's men has finished the job I should have done.

The job I couldn't do when I saw the censure in Bianca's expression.

I look over his shoulder toward Danelli who meets my gaze squarely, but there are questions in his shadowed face. Questions I cannot answer at this time.

Why did I not shoot them dead already? Why am I standing here, seemingly at a loss, instead of taking control as I normally do, in any situation, no matter how dire? Why am I hesitating when I should be the most decisive I have ever been in my life?

Why is my mind on Bianca, when it should be firmly fixed on the business at hand?

Even if Danelli voices none of his concerns in front of everyone else, I sense his doubt. I feel it within myself.

My family was attacked, on more than one front. Some of them may even now be dead or dying.

And it will be up to me to avenge them.

Rossi will discover that this war between us, that he no doubt thought would be finished today, has only just begun.

And it is now kill or be killed, because if not, Bianca and my child could be caught in the cross fire.

"If you gaze long enough into an abyss, the abyss will gaze back into you."
Friedrich Nietzsche

Bianca

BY THE TIME I arrive at the marina with Matteo, and we go through the rigmarole of checking for danger before he hustles me on board, my brain is working again. Sort of.

Though my nerves are shot and my hands won't stop shaking.

Rio called this his boat, but it's more like a fancy super-yacht than a boat. At least, to my non-boating mind.

I follow Matteo downstairs, below deck I guess it's called, and he shows me to a private cabin area that contains both a bedroom and a living area.

"Wait here in the saloon for Rio. Make yourself at home,

Mrs. Agosti. There are drinks at the bar if you need it." He indicates a button on the wall near the door. "Press that if you need anything at all. The only people aboard are Rio's most trusted staff."

"All right." I wrap my arms around my middle. "Thank you, Matteo."

He turns to leave, but I call him back. "Can you please let me know if you hear anything about those at the estate? Especially, well...Francine?"

He studies me silently for a moment, then nods. "If I'm allowed, then yes. I will let you know."

If he's allowed? I guess working for Rio means no one does anything without the Boss's permission.

"That's fair enough. Thank you. And please, call me Bianca in the future."

He inclines his head, and this time I let him leave, and then I sink onto one of the lounge chairs and lean over my knees, fighting the urge to throw up.

Every time I close my eyes, I see death. Bits of brain matter flying everywhere. Bone fragments. Blood. So much blood.

So instead, I keep my eyes open, blinking as little as possible, and stare at the carpet beneath my feet. Luxurious pile. Looks soft. I slide my heels off and test it out, wriggling my toes. It is as soft as it looks.

But this almost-white color isn't practical in the Mafia world. They'd never get the blood out if death were to come calling here, too.

Eventually, I sit up and lean back against the couch. How can I justify bringing a child into this world? How will I ever tell him or her that their father is a monster? A murderer?

At least he acknowledges who and what he is. And at

least he does it with purpose—to maintain his empire and keep his family safe.

What's my excuse? I love him, and as much as I hate who he is and what he stands for, that love has not dissipated.

I thought it would, after what happened tonight.

During the drive here to the marina, I poked and prodded at my feelings, assuming the love would be gone. That I would feel only revulsion and hatred and that the need to get away—to run far and fast—would rear up once again in my thoughts.

The revulsion is there. It sits in my gut, roiling with acid. Human life should not be so little valued. Even though it was clear that Anders was about to kill Rio, and that was a definite case of kill or be killed, that doesn't explain the others.

I hate what he is with every cell in my body. But the love is still there, despite that. I want him, even now. I want his arms around me. I want his cock deep inside me as we rut and fuck and forget for a few minutes about the horror of what just happened. The horror of living this life.

And I *hate* that I feel this way, *more* than I hate him.

What does that make me?

Perhaps I am just as much a monster as he is. More so, maybe, because I wasn't born to this life. I was raised to have a different set of morals. I should know better.

But you were *born to this life, Bianca.* The traitorous inner voice intrudes and will not go away.

You were born a Mafia princess, and this life is in your blood.

I remember the little white card that the agent Felicity handed me all those weeks ago. I don't believe she's FBI. I do think she genuinely works in some kind of law enforcement agency, but I'm not certain which one. Regardless, the card is long gone, torn into tiny pieces and flushed away down the toilet. But I memorized the number before I destroyed the evidence of possible betrayal.

I could call that number right now, if I wanted, before Rio returns. Before more of his staff invade my personal space and take away my ability to do anything without constant scrutiny.

I could save my child from a future of violence and death by making that call. But in doing so, I would condemn my child's father to a life in prison.

I know what I *should* do. But I don't yet know what I *will* do.

And in that fact right there, I realize that I am far more monstrous than my crime boss husband ever was or will be.

Rio

I AM uncertain what to expect when I enter the saloon. Will Bianca shoot those judgmental eyes my way? Is she still in shock, unable to process what happened earlier? Has she been tipped over the edge into madness?

The suite is quiet, the saloon empty. I frown and head through into the bedroom. She is lying awake in the middle of the bed, curled up on her side with her arms wrapped around her knees. She has showered—her hair splayed out across the pillows is loose and wet—and donned a thick white robe. Her feet are bare, and she looks younger than usual with her makeup-free face and that sprinkling of freckles across her nose that give her an innocent air.

She is innocent no more. Not after tonight.

Slowly, she turns her head to meet my gaze. No shock remains in her features, nor any sign of madness. She is simply quiet, studying me with an expression I cannot read.

"Will you please shower, Rio? And then join me."

I take a step closer to the bed, but she holds up a hand.

"No. I need you to shower. Please. Don't..." Her hand drops down, and her grip around her knees tightens. "Do not come near me until you've showered. Scrub yourself. A lot."

"All right. But we need to talk, Bianca."

"Yes. We do."

I want to say more. I want to think of some words that will comfort her. But I don't know what to say or how to do that. I've never comforted anyone before. Never had the need, or the desire.

She turns her face away from me, into the pillow, and after a few more seconds in which I struggle to find words, I simply leave her there and head to the shower to wash off the last remnants of the attack.

I don't bother dressing after. I need to feel my wife, skin on skin. When I return, Bianca seems to be of the same mind. She has removed her robe and is lying on her back, naked.

She opens her arms, and her breasts jut upward, her nipples puckered and pointing. Then she drops her legs wide, her knees bent to display the pink folds of her cunt. She's already wet and ready.

My cock hardens instantly at the sight.

"Hold me, please, Rio." Her voice breaks on my name. She swallows convulsively before clearing her throat. Then she lifts her chin. "Fuck me. Make me forget."

Bianca

Rio is on me within seconds, his lips crashing against mine and his hands seemingly everywhere at once as he settles his hips between my open legs. His flesh is already rigid, pressing against my belly as he grinds into me.

I groan at the sensation that rolls out from our connection. Wanting more. Needing more. Needing it all.

I can't believe I'm doing this. Wanting sex after such a horrific event. But I crave Rio. I need him more than I ever have. I want his strength, his power, his *possession*, like I've never wanted it before.

I writhe beneath him, giving in to impulse and letting thought drift away. I arch up when strong fingers pinch at one of my nipples, twisting the nub to the point of pain.

"Yes," I cry out between clenched teeth. "More!"

He bends his head and pulls my breast into his mouth, licking and laving and biting down on the flesh. I shudder at the pain and moan some more, knowing I'll have bite marks tomorrow.

It's not enough. It will never be enough.

He gets off on my pain. And since meeting Rio, I know I do, too.

I run my hands over hard muscle and silken skin, digging my fingernails in deeply when I reach his back. Lashing out. Marking him. *Mine*.

He grunts and raises his head, staring down at me with eyes so dark and intense I know I will never see the bottom of that pool of blackness within him.

What does he see? Do I have the same blackness within me?

Are we the same, me and Rio?

Abruptly, he flips me over onto my stomach before lifting my bottom and smacking me. The sting is sudden and sharp and brings instant tears to my eyes. He does it again, and I let out an involuntary squeal. Despite the shock and the pain, I lift my ass higher, wanting more.

I *need* more. I need it all. So I can forget.

"*Fuck* me!" I can barely get words out; my voice is so hoarse and full of desire. "God, Rio, please. Give me oblivion. After today, give me that at least."

There is no thought left after that, only instinct. No more foreplay, only fucking.

He grips my hips and then shoves inside me in one hard thrust. I rock back against him, writhing on his cock, urging him to go faster, harder, to *destroy* me...

"Fuck, Bianca. Fuck, woman. I need you. So fucking bad..." His rhythm falters, becomes erratic, and his flesh inside me grows impossibly larger. Harder. *Perfect*.

The orgasm rises within me, not clitoral but from deep inside. It coils, and grows, and rolls out like a tsunami wave right through my body until I can't hold it in any longer, and I scream and buck uncontrollably beneath him as the force of my release takes me over the edge.

Vaguely, I hear his roar behind me and feel his shudders and the hot spurting heat within as he tumbles with me over the cliff edge into climax.

But even as my body convulses along with Rio and I continue to pray for oblivion, the gruesome images of blood and gore and staring dead eyes remain imprinted on my mind and burned into my memory.

"It is impossible to underestimate the significance of your today's choices."
Gautama Buddha

Bianca

"YOU'RE certain you are pregnant, Bianca?" He strokes my stomach in the aftermath of our lovemaking, his touch light and so full of love that I can't stop the tears that well in my eyes.

How can I reconcile this hand, cradling me so delicately, with the one that held a gun—that *killed* people—only a few short hours ago?

And yet it is the same hand; the same man. The monster *is* the man I love.

I don't know what to do.

I'm lying to myself in this moment. Of course I know what to do.

Call Felicity. Call the agent. And get out, for the sake of your baby.

I link my fingers with his on my belly, sadness overwhelming me. "I think so. I did a home test which was positive. I guess I'll need a blood test to be sure, but…yes."

"You have made me very happy with this news."

His fingertips trace my abdomen, and the tiniest smile plays about his lips as he leans in and places a tender kiss on my shoulder.

I roll away from him slightly, not wanting him to look at me when my tears begin to fall, but he rolls me back to face him. There is no hiding from Rio. Not even in this moment when I'm terrified that may have been the last time we ever make love.

When I'm even more terrified he may discover that I'm considering running.

"Did you kill those men, Rio, after I left? The ones who worked for Rossi."

He simply stares at me intently as if trying to read my mind.

"You're not going to answer that question, are you?"

His brows come together. "You should not be involved with that side of things." He rolls onto his back, raising up his arms and tucking them beneath his head on the pillow. "I will arrange for you to see our family physician as soon as possible. Normally, he would come out to see you at the estate, but…"

The estate. "Is everyone out there okay? What happened? Is…" I stop as he begins to shake his head and his mouth thins.

My heart lurches almost to a stop before launching into a faster than usual beat.

"No," he says. "There was a simultaneously timed attack at the estate as well as the club. My brother is fine, as is Tommaso."

"But…Francine…" Tears clog my throat. I already know what he's going to say.

"My aunt is dead."

The tone seems cold and impersonal, but I know him better now. I hear the undercurrent of raw pain in that simple statement.

"God, Rio, I'm so sorry." I reach out and wrap my arms around him, and we lie like that for several minutes in silence.

Eventually, he sucks in a ragged breath and releases it slowly. "They tell me she stepped in front of Nicky. Stopped the bullet meant for him, apparently. She died for her family, and that act of bravery will never be forgotten."

Abruptly, he rolls out of bed and leaves the room, heading out to the saloon area. I hear the clink of ice and then the sound of liquid pouring into glass.

I lie on my back and stare up at the timber-lined ceiling, wrapping my arms around my middle to ward off a sudden chill.

Poor Francine. I didn't love her, but she didn't deserve that. No one does.

And yet, it seems as if violence and death is a regular occurrence in this life.

I can't do this anymore. I can't.

A shrill ring sounds nearby, causing me to jump, my heart rate accelerating again before I realize it is simply Rio's cell phone. He answers quickly, and I sit up and dangle my legs over the bed, intending to go have another shower.

I was in the bathroom earlier for over half an hour, beneath a spray of water so hot it was painful, but it was as if I could not get the stench of blood and death off me. I know it's just in my mind. I washed and scrubbed myself until my skin hurt. I can't possibly have any trace of blood on me. But still… I shiver. Another shower won't hurt.

Rio's voice rises slightly in the saloon, its cadence changing to one of annoyance. "…with Carbone dead, we'll have to launder another way. Get Carnarvon to look at…"

The voice fades, and with it, my sense of dread grows. I jump off the bed and rush into the bathroom.

I don't want to hear it. I don't want to hear anything that may tempt me to give him up. But now I can't unhear it.

We'll have to launder another way.

I turn on the water as hot as I can tolerate it and slide beneath the spray, praying yet again for some kind of oblivion from the moral quagmire that my life has somehow become.

THE NEXT AFTERNOON, I pace back and forth in the saloon, my cell phone in hand as I try to gather the courage to make the call I know has to be made.

My husband or my child.

That's what this moment comes down to, and in the end, it is no choice at all. I knew what I would have to do the moment I stared into Rio's eyes that night as he stood over those poor, doomed men.

He trusts me—not much, but then, he doesn't trust anyone much. And yet, there is a softening within him, at least when it comes to me. I see it in his eyes when he looks at me. He is beginning to care for me, and I don't believe he has ever let himself feel for another woman like this.

It just makes what I'm about to do even worse. It feels like the ultimate act of betrayal.

My nausea is so bad I've been unable to keep anything down all day. I can't tell if the roiling sickness in my stomach is from the pregnancy hormones or from stress at the knowledge I'm about to betray my husband.

Rio is out somewhere today, meeting with Tommaso to finalize the funeral arrangements for his aunt.

I clutch my phone. I have to call her. Felicity. It's that or bring my child up to become just like his father. Immune to violence and death and steeped in immorality.

I am about to punch in the number when I receive a text message from an unknown caller.

My heart jumps into my mouth when I read the words on the screen.

Anders was acting unsanctioned. I would never want to hurt you, my dear. I want you safe, at all costs. Please believe me. I would never hurt Rina's daughter.

Rossi? I sink onto the couch, my legs trembling so hard I don't think they'll hold me up. Is this a trick? Is he using me to send a message to Rio? To try and stop any revenge attack on his own family? Knowing Rio, there will be revenge, and I am certain it will be far more violent than what occurred the other night.

I read the message again. What if he's genuine? I never had the sense from Rossi that he meant me any harm. What if he's telling the truth? What if Anders *was* acting without permission from Rossi?

A glimmer of an idea forms, and I tap the phone against my cheek as I think.

What if there's a way to escape this violent world but avoid betraying Rio in the process?

Could it work?

Do I have the strength to use Rossi's connection to my mother to evade not only Rio, but the Feds as well?

Quickly, I send back a reply text, asking Rossi to call me. Fifteen excruciatingly long minutes later, he does.

"Bianca, my dear. Will you pass on to Rio that—"

"Please, Carlos, listen." My heart races and my hands tremble.

Rossi is silent, then finally, he says, "Yes?" The kind uncle tone is gone.

"I promise I will let Rio know what you said about Anders. But in return, I need your help."

"With what?"

"To disappear."

Following that phone call, I remain seated for some time, terrified at what I've just set in motion. My legs would not hold me up if I were to try and stand right now.

When the lights automatically come on above my head in the ceiling of the saloon, I realize it must be getting dark outside. Rio will likely be back soon.

I am out of time. The decision has been made, and the die has been cast.

Taking a deep breath, I release it in a rush, and then I lift my phone once again and punch in the number I've had burned into my memory since the night of the gala ball.

"Betrayal is the only truth that sticks."
Arthur Miller

Rio

THERE IS no trace of the bloodbath that occurred here in my
club only three weeks ago. The firm's cleanup crew is first-
rate, as are the construction workers and repairmen on our
books. Other than the closure of the club for a couple of days,
it is as if the attack by Rossi's people never happened at all.

And yet it did, and that moment changed everything. I
had revenge in mind to weed out the killer of my parents, and
I planned to use Carlos Rossi to flush out the perpetrator.

Now, old vengeance can wait. New vengeance has taken
its place.

Rossi's men attempted to hurt my wife and the child

growing in her belly. They *killed* my aunt. Nothing will stand in the way of my retribution. Rossi is firmly in my sights.

I am not concerned at this point about the police. I have long known it is of benefit to have law enforcement on your payroll, and as a consequence, their investigation into the shooting incident was brief.

I am seated in my office above the club, listening to the low thrum of music from downstairs. It isn't late, but since it's Friday evening, the music starts early to capture the work crowd who want to party a little before heading home from the city.

None of them seem to know—or care—that multiple bodies were removed from the very floor on which they now dance.

That night—as Bianca told me she was carrying my child—I lost my aunt in the attack on the estate. We buried Francine in the family plot just out of the city in a service attended by hundreds. Tommaso has ordered an elaborate monument to mark her final resting place with honor. When the monument is ready, we will hold another, smaller ceremony with only immediate family in attendance.

I lean back in the chair, unaccountably weary. For a moment, I wonder what it would be like to have been born a second or third son, and not the eldest. Or even to have been born into another family altogether, outside this life in the business.

What would it feel like to not have the weight of a whole organization riding on your shoulders? Would I be different? Less inclined to feed the darkness that lies within me? Would I be more suitable for one such as Bianca?

Two innocents together in a life that includes blinkers on and naïveté intact.

Would that be a satisfying life? Or would the boredom of living within the law—living with convention—be our downfall? Would my dark side crave fulfilment regardless of my blood?

I know how Bianca feels about me. I sense the complexity and ambiguity of her emotions every time we're in the same room. Her beautiful brown eyes cannot lie.

Part of me regrets bringing her into this life, but that other, baser side revels in the fact that the woman I initially thought would need to be eliminated has somehow ended up capturing my heart and taking her place by my side.

Frivolous thoughts. Useless. I need to get back to work. I swivel the chair and pour myself a whiskey from the crystal decanter I keep behind me, and then turn back to resume reading the contract in front of me.

I lift the document, but have only taken one sip of the amber liquid when a commotion breaks out beyond the office door. Yelling and scuffling, a mix of male and female voices. I place the glass carefully on the desk and reach down beneath the desktop to rest my hand on the gun secured beneath. The muzzle points toward the door. Whoever enters will be dead in seconds if they try to harm or attack me.

"No, I'm sorry. Stop! You can't—"

The door bursts open, and a bunch of strangers tumble into the office, followed by my secretary Dana, who always works late on Fridays, and three of my security team. My hand on the gun trigger relaxes, but only slightly.

I can tell immediately that these strangers are law enforcement. Two men and one woman, neatly dressed and all of whom have an air about them of watchful eagerness. Probably federal rather than local, I surmise. The signs are unmistakable once you know what to look for.

The woman steps forward, waving a paper around in the air before plonking it down in front of me. "Gregorio Agosti, we have a warrant to search these premises."

I don't look down at the document. Instead, I stare intently at her, familiarity rearing up, and my heart gives a strange thud, almost as if it has just missed a beat.

I know her.

Or at least, I recognize her. She's the blonde who was in the bathroom with Bianca at the gala ball several weeks ago. The night my gut told me something was off. But I was so focused on Bianca that I ignored my instinct about anything being wrong.

The woman goes on with more waffle, but I tune her out, trying to control my shock.

What is Bianca's role in this woman's presence in my office? Does she *have* a role? Is she aware that these people are our enemy?

Did she send them here to bring me down in retaliation for kidnapping her and removing her from her former life? Has she been playing a long game, toying with me, reeling me in with her innocent sexuality and her promise of forever through our child?

No. I cannot believe that of her. Bianca would not betray me in such a monstrous fashion. Not when she's carrying my baby. Not when she looks at me the way she does, with love —however reluctant—in her expression.

I relinquish my hold fully on the gun and lean back in my chair with folded arms. They will find the gun when they search, of course. Together with other weapons stashed throughout the building.

But my legal team has always ensured I have the necessary papers and licenses for everything in this office—and the club downstairs, for that matter. Right down to the last pen or bottle of wine.

They won't find anything incriminating here.

Danelli rushes in at this point, obviously alerted by one of his men. I hold up a hand, slowing his impetus.

"You may search," I tell the woman slowly, "but if you damage one single thing in this building, I will bill your department for the cost."

"A threat, Agosti?" One of the male agents steps forward, belligerence in his tone and stance.

So predictable. So ineffectual.

I raise an eyebrow in his direction. "No. A fact."

The woman frowns at her colleague, surreptitiously waving him back. She speaks into an earpiece, telling the rest of the search team to come on up and get started.

I ignore them all then and turn to Danelli. "Get Carnarvon up here now. I'll meet him in the club."

Carnarvon and his team of lawyers are on retainer, and there is no one I trust more in a situation like this to ensure I come out unscathed. Their firm occupies office space on the first floor of this building, so I expect it will be less than five minutes before my lawyer or his representative is seated beside me in the club.

"Yes, Boss." Danelli scurries from the room, already lifting his cell phone to his ear.

My secretary is next to receive instruction. "Get Bianca on the line for me. I will speak with her shortly." At Dana's nod, I turn finally to Matteo, one of the team who happens to be on duty tonight. "Watch them. Make sure they don't break anything or take anything they are not supposed to. Remind them I will sue if they go outside the bounds of the warrant."

Without looking again at the blonde or her offsiders, I leave the room and head downstairs to my club.

"No one can find Bianca, sir."

My secretary has arrived in the club only a minute behind Carnarvon and two of his cronies. Carnarvon is in the process of taking a seat and laying his briefcase on the low table in front of the couches when he pauses at Dana's announcement.

Her usually immaculate and calm face is set in unaccustomed lines of worry.

I blink a couple of times, trying to process what she's just said. "That's impossible. What the fuck do you mean, no one can find her? She's on the boat with a whole security detail watching over her. She can't have disappeared without them knowing. *Find* her!"

"They can't." Dana's fingers twist together. She knows my dark side and clearly doesn't want it directed at her. "They've looked everywhere. Scoured the whole boat. She appears to be…gone."

Fury and fear fill me in equal measure. Did Rossi get to her somehow? Did I not leave enough security in place? Is my wife—and my baby—dead?

"Find her," I grind out through clenched teeth. "Now."

I snatch at my cell phone lying on the table and punch in Bianca's number. It goes straight through to voice mail. I end the call and try again. Then again.

As it connects for a third time to voice mail, I spy the blonde agent striding confidently in front of the bar on her way over to our cluster of people. A growl erupts from my throat at the sight of her, and I am as close as I've ever been to losing complete control. I turn my back on her and speak urgently into the phone, putting every ounce of command that I have into the message.

"Bianca. Call me now. I don't care where you are or what you're doing. *Call. Me. Now.*"

I hang up and take a moment to breathe. I cannot lose it in front of these agents. I cannot lose it in front of anyone. I am the Boss.

I need to get it together and act like the Boss. Dangerous. Emotionless. Logical and reasoning. If I don't, someone else will step up and take my place, and the Agosti name will be ground into dust.

I do a reasonable job of clawing back control of my temper. Reasonable, until I turn back and my gaze meets that of the blonde woman.

She smirks at me, a knowing look in her eyes. "You need to come with us now, Gregorio. Though I should confirm you are not under arrest. Yet."

"Then he does not need to go anywhere with you." Carnarvon's dry tone cuts across the sudden silence.

She ignores him, skewering me with a look that chills my blood. "You won't ever find her, you know. Don't bother looking. We have Bree somewhere safe, and you will never get to her again."

I suck in a breath, and then release it slowly. *They. Have. Bree? No, not Bree.* "My wife's name is Bianca."

I rise to my feet, the sounds around me warping and distorting. Vaguely, I hear Dana's gasp and Carnarvon calling my name, then shouts and screams as the black mist takes me.

I lift the table and launch it across the room into the bar.

"One can run away from anything but oneself."
Stefan Zweig

Bianca

THE BUS PULLS out of the depot in a cloud of fumes and a roar of noise, and I sink down into my seat, hoping I look like any other traveler who doesn't have the funds to go by air.

I adjust my light-brown wig, hoping it doesn't look too fake. With colored contact lenses turning my eyes blue, and in these old jeans, T-shirt, and with a worn backpack slung onto the empty seat beside me, I don't think I look like Bianca Carlotti at all. I don't even look like Bree Walker. Not anymore. Bree is long gone, and Bianca will hopefully sink into oblivion as soon as I hit Augusta.

Oblivion. I begged Rio to take me there that night, and for a time in his arms, he almost succeeded in delivering me into its welcome embrace. But the memories and nightmares always return. Violence and death haunt me. Oblivion is fleeting. Unless, of course, I choose the finality of death.

I curl my fingers over my belly. It is just starting to round out a little now, and the nausea is growing as each day progresses. That's a good thing, from what I've read. It means the hormones are strong and the baby has a chance at surviving. I wonder if stress is making the nausea worse. There is certainly a lot of that rolling through my body.

Every time we stop and some passengers get on and off, I have to fight to control my breathing. Sweat coats my armpits and drips down my back, and then we roll again, and no one seems to be paying me attention.

Until one particular stop, somewhere near Portsmouth, I think, and a dark-suited guy climbs aboard. Who wears a suit on a bus? Is he here for me? I tense as he seems to study the passengers one by one. His gaze alights on me, and I hold my breath, trying not to meet his eyes.

Praying he won't come near me. Praying he isn't one of Rio's men. Or one of Rossi's. Or a Fed.

He starts down the aisle, reaches me, and passes by. I'm too scared to turn my head to watch where he ends up, but I hear the scratch of clothing and the squeak of the fake leather as he slides into a seat somewhere on the opposite side of me.

The bus takes off, and I wait, holding in my whimpers by sheer will alone. When nothing happens, I finally gather the courage to shoot a glance behind me. The guy is slumped against the window, eyes closed and mouth half open, already asleep.

He's not interested in me.

Not a Mafia goon, then.

Oh, thank God. Thank God.

Eventually, I relax the tiniest bit, but I still can't sleep. I am too close to the edge, always on alert. I hope I can settle soon when I reach wherever I'm going and give this child a better start than living on nerves and adrenaline.

That old life will never change, but my new life has to be different.

Canada, here I come. By way of Augusta, Maine, if all goes according to plan.

My plan. Not the Feds'. And damn sure not Rossi's plan. Felicity and her team never got the chance beyond an initial debriefing meeting to whisk me away into hiding. Rossi got there first.

He's the one who provided me with cash and fake ID documentation, but he thinks I'm stopping in Augusta. He has an apartment already lined up there for me to move right on in.

But I have no intention of leaving one monster crime lord for another. There would be no point to leaving Rio at all if I were simply to allow Rossi to step into his place as my protector. Or my jailer.

No. From this day onward, I rely on no one but myself for protection. I am strong enough to do this on my own. I have to be, for my own survival and that of my child. No one is going to get in my way.

Only, for every mile the bus travels away from Rio, away from danger, it also takes me farther from the man who stole my heart and claimed my soul.

And my heart breaks just a little bit more each time.

Rio

IT TOOK Carnarvon and his team less than four hours to get me out of the agency's interview room and back here to my office. Danelli has swept the place for bugs, and I have been assured it is clean. At least for now.

When I tell them all to leave me, Carnarvon pauses at the door. The pity in his expression as he stares at me almost costs him his life. I am teetering that close to the edge.

"I can confirm their tip-off came from your wife, sir," he says.

"About the botched Carbone deal? The shootings?" Of course it would be about the shootings. The horror in her eyes that day has never really left her.

I should have seen that; protected against its negative effects. But when it comes to Bianca, I have always been blind, it would seem.

"Yes, and no. The Carbone deal, but not the shootings."

That surprises me. I tilt my head in my lawyer's direction. "Go on."

"The money laundering. They're looking for evidence you used the Carbone deal to funnel dirty money."

"Ah. Easier for them to prove, I expect, than a mass shooting where there are no bodies, no bullets or casings, and no blood."

"Indeed."

"Go."

Carnarvon shuffles his feet, the hesitation raising my ire. I notice for the first time a small white envelope in his hand. I stare at him, and he swallows before darting forward to lay the envelope on my desk.

"This came for you today."

It is from her. I can almost smell her scent rising up from the missive, even though I know it must be pure imagination.

"Get out. Now."

This time Carnarvon complies, fear tightening his jawline as he retreats, leaving me alone to brood on the betrayal by my wife. The only woman—the only person—with whom I have ever let down my guard.

I stride to the sideboard and pour myself a whiskey, staring down into the amber liquid and thinking about love and family, betrayal and revenge.

And the rage rises up, and up, until I can no longer think; until I can no longer see the drink in my hand. The black mist, as my father used to call it when it took me, obscures my vision, my hearing, my every sense.

I open my mouth and roar, allowing all the anger and hurt to rush out of me in a torrent. And then I let go and destroy the office around me.

Afterward, I perch on the only unbroken piece of furniture in the space—the high-backed leather chair that used to sit behind my desk.

The desk itself is in pieces, as is everything else in the once-cavernous and always stylish room. Now it is littered with shards of crystal and glass and bits of broken timber. The shelves that held papers and books are skewed sideways or tipped over across the carpet. Artwork is on the floor. The mirror above the mantel opposite the floor-to-ceiling windows is now heavily cracked.

I study my warped reflection, feeling nothing when my distorted face stares back at me.

Nothing but the cold rage still burning deep down inside.

She betrayed me.

She. Betrayed. *Me*.

I see the white envelope peeking up from the rubble, resting atop a picture frame on the floor. I bend down, reaching into the mess, and pull out both the missive and the framed photograph that previously sat on my desk. A wedding photo of Bianca and me, snapped as we were leaving the chapel.

I open the envelope and pull out the single sheet of paper inside. The words blur as I read, and I scrub at my eyes to clear them. I will never allow myself to cry. Ever. Over anything.

Rio, you must hate me now. I'm so sorry. You need to know that Carlos Rossi was not aware of the attacks until afterward. Anders was working on his own, without permission from his boss.

I will process that information later. Right now, I focus only on the last scrawled line of the note.

I love you, Rio. I always will.

The note drops to the floor as I pull the framed photo closer, studying it. She is staring up at me, her lips parted and her eyes flashing with a myriad of emotions. Love and hate. Even back then, she couldn't hide the desire; the need.

Despite her hatred for me and everything I stand for.

I prop the frame upright on the floor in front of my feet, thinking about love and hate. Desire and betrayal.

I reach into my jacket pocket for my cell phone—somehow, despite the devastation I've just inflicted on my office, I am still wearing my suit—and dial a number I know well.

"Dartside Investigations. Can I help you?"

"It is Rio."

An audible hiss at the other end confirms my name is enough introduction. "Yes, sir. How can we assist today?"

"I need someone found. A woman. The job is one of life and death. And the budget is…" I pause, considering. "The

235

budget is limitless. Whatever it takes, this woman must be found and brought to me. As a matter of supreme urgency."

Before my child is born.

I reach again beneath my jacket and this time pull out the gun that Carnarvon returned to me the moment we left the offices of the Feds.

I check. It is fully loaded. Good. Idly, I spin the chamber, looking down at the photo. The moment it was taken was a snapshot in time where I was, if not happy, at least satisfied with where my life with Bianca was headed.

Spin, click. Spin, click.

It was a time before my aunt was murdered. A time before my family was threatened. A time before my *fucking wife betrayed me*.

Spin, click.

What's a little more glass among this mess?

I cock the gun and point it at the photo, steadying the barrel, focusing on Bianca's face.

My beautiful wife. *La mia bella moglie.*

And then I pull the trigger.

I'm coming for you, little bird.

I hope you enjoyed book one of the *Dark Enemies* trilogy.
The series continues in book two, *Ruthless Betrayal.*

RUTHLESS BETRAYAL
DARK ENEMIES BOOK TWO

Blurb

MY HUSBAND IS on the hunt, and I am his prey.

I was innocent, once upon a time. Then a monster kidnapped me, and I was reinvented as a mob boss's wife.

I fled to protect myself and my child, and now I live a life as far removed from Boston high society as possible.

But no-one can escape the past forever. Rio Agosti is coming for us. I feel it in my bones.

And I'm not sure I have the strength to resist his dark allure.

Read *Ruthless Betrayal*, book two in the deliciously dark enemies-to-lovers Mafia world of the *Dark Enemies* series.

ABOUT THE AUTHOR

Zoe Delaney is the dark romantic suspense pen name of *USA Today* bestselling author, Jen Katemi.

When Zoe isn't writing, she runs an editing and proofreading business, dotes on her daughters, and pampers various cats—including a rescue with one hip. She lives in Melbourne, Australia.

Find out more and sign up for Zoe's reader newsletter at **her website**:

www.zoe-delaney.com

www.ingramcontent.com/pod-product-compliance
Lightning Source LLC
Chambersburg PA
CBHW031947240626
47153CB00003B/898